Recital of the Dark Verses

Recital
of the
Dark Verses

Luis Felipe Fabre

TRANSLATED BY HEATHER CLEARY

Deep Vellum Publishing
Dallas, Texas

Deep Vellum Publishing
3000 Commerce St., Dallas, Texas 75226
deepvellum.org · @deepvellum

Deep Vellum is a 501c3 nonprofit literary arts organization
founded in 2013 with the mission to bring
the world into conversation through literature.

FIRST EDITION, 2023

LIBRARY OF CONGRESS CATALOGING-IN-PUBLICATION DATA

Names: Fabre, Luis Felipe, 1974- author. | Cleary, Heather, translator.
Title: Recital of the dark verses / Luis Felipe Fabre ; translated by
Heather Cleary.
Other titles: Declaración de las canciones oscuras. English
Description: First edition. | Dallas, Texas : Deep Vellum Publishing, 2023.
Identifiers: LCCN 2023022997 (print) | LCCN 2023022998 (ebook) | ISBN
9781646052790 (trade paperback) | ISBN 9781646053001 (ebook)
Subjects: LCSH: John of the Cross, Saint, 1542-1591--Fiction. | LCGFT:
Biographical fiction. | Picaresque fiction. | Novels.
Classification: LCC PQ7298.16.A324 D4313 2023 (print) | LCC PQ7298.16.A324
(ebook) | DDC 863/.64--dc23/eng/20230524
LC record available at https://lccn.loc.gov/2023022997
LC ebook record available at https://lccn.loc.gov/2023022998

ISBN (TPB) 978-1-64605-279-0 | ISBN (Ebook) 978-1-64605-300-1

Support for this publication has been provided in part by the National Endowment for the
Arts, the Texas Commission on the Arts, the City of Dallas Office of Arts and Culture, and the
George and Fay Young Foundation.

Cover design by Alban Fischer

Interior layout and typesetting by KGT

PRINTED IN THE UNITED STATES OF AMERICA

Reciting the *Recital*

When tracing translation's etymological roots, it is easy to get caught up in the carryings-over of empires and educations, overlooking one of *translatio*'s quirkier cousins: the solemn conveyance of Catholic relics—for example, the (illicit) translation from Úbeda to Segovia of (most of) the remains of the humble friar who would become the great San Juan de la Cruz.

Luis Felipe Fabre's brilliant, bawdy *Recital of the Dark Verses* centers on this posthumous transport and the misadventures of the three men charged with the task. It is the story of a heist, a road novel, a coming-of-age tale, and a raunchy slapstick comedy told in prose that sends a contemporary jolt through the flourishes of Golden Age Spanish. It is also a witty and wise commentary on the verse of one of Spain's most important poets, woven from the lines for which he is best known—a revival and regeneration of words written more than four centuries ago.

The novel begins at the doors of the monastery in

Úbeda late one night in 1592, as a bailiff of the royal court and his two aides—Ferrán, desperate to stay a few paces ahead of the Inquisition, and Diego, who over the course of their travels will stumble into a sexual awakening—prepare to expropriate Fray Juan's remains in a humble leather trunk. Traveling under cover of night, the three fend off demonic visitations, carnal temptations, and an array of intrusive interlocutors driven wild by the delicate aroma of the friar's incorrupt body. Their journey is populated by a cast of characters drawn from Greek mythology, Shakespeare, and San Juan's own verse, including a wanton band of shepherds, an indiscreet innkeeper, and a blind man who sees all.

And then, of course, there's the man in the trunk. Before his veneration and translation, the Spanish mystic known in English as Saint John of the Cross is born Juan de Yepes y Álvarez in 1542. He grows up in extreme poverty after his father is disowned for marrying beneath his station but receives a basic education through the Church and joins the Carmelite Order in 1563. Young Juan then sets out to study at the fabled University of Salamanca, where he reads the Song of Songs in its translation by Fray Luis de León, who is brought before the Inquisition for that very same translation in 1571. The poem—a celebration of sensual and spiritual love—penetrates the consciousness of the future saint and becomes the motor of a contagious seduction: Juan surrenders to his desire for spiritual union with God in poems that will later spark covetous urges and strange yearnings among those who deem him holy.

After Salamanca, Juan begins to run with a more extreme crowd. In 1567, he meets Saint Teresa of Ávila, who sees in him a kindred zeal for austerity and invites him to join her movement to reform the Carmelite Order, which, to her mind, has grown lamentably lax. Among the injunctions she wishes to revive are those forbidding meat, speaking, robes made of soft cloth, and shoes that cover the toes. (Based on the latter particularity, this new order comes to be known as the Discalced, or barefoot, Carmelites.) So dedicated is Fray Juan to these austere principles that in 1577 he is taken prisoner by a group of Carmelites who find him too fervent in his faith, too ascetic in his tastes. He is starved, flogged, and confined to a tiny cell in the monastery at Toledo for many months—until, as the story goes, his door is left ajar one pitch-dark night and he makes his escape, climbing naked down the outer wall of the monastery on the "secret stair" of a rope of braided cloth.

After recovering from this ordeal and setting to paper the verses he had composed and memorized while in captivity, Fray Juan returns to establishing Discalced chapters around Spain. His efforts are so successful that in 1588 he is named prior at Segovia, but he stirs the pot again by criticizing the vicar general, and in 1590 he is sent as punishment to La Peñuela, an isolated monastery in Andalucía. There he falls ill with erysipelas and is transported to the Discalced monastery in Úbeda, where he dies covered in sores on December 14, 1591. His final request is to hear the Song of Songs.

What follows is something of a blur: historians disagree about which limbs ended up where, and when. What is known is that Fray Juan's remains caused much commotion among the townspeople of Úbeda, who thronged to venerate the body and snatch whatever small relics they could. And that doña Ana de Peñalosa, sister of the powerful don Luis de Mercado, sent messengers to bring Fray Juan back to the Discalced monastery she funded in Segovia, leading to what can only be described as a tug of war over his body in which the pope eventually needed to intervene as referee. In the process, Fray Juan—who would not be canonized until 1726—loses unquantified snippets and all his limbs to reliquaries in Úbeda, Madrid, and finally Segovia, where his head and torso rest today.

In *Recital of the Dark Verses*, Fabre draws on three of the saint's best-known poems: "On a Dark Night" (the centerpiece of the novel), "Love's Living Flame," and the "Spiritual Canticle," which was composed while the friar was imprisoned and describes—in the first person—the desperate search across hill and dale of a bride (the soul) for her bridegroom (God). Fray Juan also wrote his escape from captivity into "On a Dark Night," while "Love's Living Flame" would come several years later: the friar wrote that poem and its commentary in 1584 at the request of the same Ana de Peñalosa who would later lay claim to his corpse.

These poems are remarkably sensual, both in their content and in the texture of their language. Indeed, they could be read as variations on the Song of Songs inscribed on the friar's own body. In all three, the soul's union with God is unabashedly coital, and in two the speaker is explicitly gendered as female—qualities that are hotly debated and steamily enacted in the pages of Fabre's novel. The eight-stanza "Night," for example, begins with the speaker—afflicted and aflame with love—taking advantage of the fact that everyone in her house is asleep to sneak out under cover of darkness:

> En una noche oscura,
> con ansias, en amores inflamada,
> ¡oh dichosa ventura!,
> salí sin ser notada
> estando ya mi casa sosegada.

In the stanzas that follow, she is guided by a light burning in her heart to a place where her Beloved awaits; they are "joined" and he falls asleep with his head on her breast as she strokes his hair. This is no solemn paean to Catholic doctrine—it is a ditty hummed by a besotted teen. Of all the options at his disposal, Fray Juan chose a popular structure and a colloquial register to evoke mystical enlightenment; the poem, though it deals with weighty ecclesiastical matters, is itself light as air. Meanwhile, the explanation of how sensual union stands in for spiritual transcendence appears in the saint's extensive prose commentaries, or *declaraciones*, in which individual lines or phrases of the poems are expounded in minute and often ineffable detail.

In a playful yet rigorous nod to this exegetic tradition, the entire text of *Recital of the Dark Verses* is a commentary on the poems of San Juan de la Cruz that centers and celebrates their rich imagery, the philosophical dimensions of their language, and their intrinsic queerness. Following the formal structure of the commentary, each chapter of the novel is introduced by a descriptive text that cites a line from one of the three poems mentioned above; in the chapter that follows, our beleaguered protagonists enact or recite or reflect upon some aspect of that line (often quite comically), and other phrases or images from the poems make cameo appearances. In this way, San Juan's verse is, through and through, the motor and material of Fabre's novel.

Weaving a compelling work of fiction from centuries-old verse is truly a prodigious feat—one that earned Fabre the prestigious Elena Poniatowska Prize in Mexico. Carrying this conceit into English added yet another layer of complexity. (Several, really.) After a long search for existing translations of San Juan that would suit the project, I realized I would need to retranslate all of "On a Dark Night" and "Love's Living Flame" (both of which are recited in full at different points in the novel), along with large sections of the "Canticle." For one thing, the English versions of the poems needed to align with Fabre's interpretation of the originals, or significant moments in the plot would no longer make sense. Retranslation was also necessary because the rhyme and meter of San Juan's verse are so important to both how the friar constructs meaning and how Fabre engages with his poems; I needed to make my own set of

English versions that at least gestured toward their lightness of gait and sensuality.

But it is not only the content of San Juan's poems that makes its way into this novel: Fabre also carries their spirit into the present day by writing *Recital* in a prose that is lithe, tactile, and transgressive. The Spanish original employs archaic verb forms and syntax—specifically, the gesture of attaching pronouns to the end of conjugated verbs—which gives the text Golden Age flair while remaining perfectly intelligible. These exact tools were not available in English, so I chose to play with word order, an antiquated past tense, and a few lexical choices here and there in order to create similar rhythmic effects, shift the temporality of the narrative without sacrificing clarity, and evoke the ludic sensibility that pervades the original. Just like the bodies tumbling together in orgiastic delight at various moments in the novel, words clatter and bounce off one another in copious linguistic couplings, breaking free of their purely descriptive function.

This erotics of language is no mere adornment, as delightful an adornment as it would be. It becomes an explicit element of the plot and goes right to the heart of Fabre's engagement with the mystic poet. At one point during a long lunch in Mexico City—where topics of discussion ranged from San Juan and Sor Juana to John Donne and Tom Stoppard's *Rosencrantz and Guildenstern Are Dead*—Fabre paused mid-thought. "In all his poems," he said, "San Juan is translating the untranslatable." The friar was keenly aware that his words would never capture the sensation of spiritual union with his god, but he kept trying. Line after line after line. Poetry, Fabre went on, is always like this. The words are never enough; at the same time the poem is an experience unto itself, it also remits us to something beyond the page. The faith he described that day is not unlike the faith of translation. To read a translation is to believe in its vital connection to something just beyond what the eye can see, a willing suspension of disbelief.

With this edition, then, San Juan de la Cruz is triply translated: the translation of his remains has been translated into the raucous plot of a novel; his mystic poems have been translated into the weft and warp of Fabre's mischievous prose; and all that translation has been translated into English. As I write this, I'm already beginning to miss working with the exquisite language of this novel and wrangling the pieces of what often felt like a three-dimensional jigsaw puzzle. I'll also miss spending time with these three "devil-sent pilferers," who come to life so fully on the page. I'm grateful to Will Evans and the team at Deep Vellum for believing in this project and helping to bring it into the world; to Diego, for illuminating every step of this journey; and to Fabre, for writing this extraordinary novel, for trusting me to translate it, and for the immense luxury of the conversations we've had along the way.

Heather Cleary
New York City, February 2023

Prologue to the *Recital of the Verses*

Ferrán?

What?

Are you still here?

What do you think?

Do you see anything?

No, nothing. You?

I know not.

What do you mean, you know not? Do you see anything, or don't you?

I know not if I see something or nothing in this darkness. I know not if what I see is the dark of night or if I
see not the night and instead wander blind through the
darkness.

How do you know it is night?

How's that?

If you know not whether you see or don't see, how do
you know it is night?

Even the blind can tell night from day.

How's that?

I know not.

Then blind you are not.

What's that?

That if you were blind you would know how to tell day from night.

What?

If you were blind, you would know the difference between seeing and not.

What's that?

That you're not blind, you're deaf.

I don't understand . . . What are you saying?

Nothing.

Nothing?

Nothing!

I just don't understand what you said about my not being blind because I can't tell day from night: it makes no sense.

You said that.

I didn't say that! Or, I didn't mean to say that . . . Or that's not how I meant it . . . Or I don't remember . . . I don't know. These shadows cloud my brain. And you? Are you certain it is night?

Nights get no more night than this. This night is like all nights together.

How do you know?

Because I'm not blind.

How do you know you're not blind?

Because I'm not blind!

I wish I were blind!

Quit your foolery.

I wish I were blind so I wouldn't need to see this terrifying darkness.

Shut your eyes, then, and your mouth.

Shut my eyes?

Shut them, we're feeling our way along as it is. Can't you see it makes no difference whether your eyes are open or closed? We've traveled so deep into the bowels of the night there's no telling the dark inside from the dark outside, or sight from lack of sight. If you wish to play the blind man, just shut your eyes. Or don't. It makes no difference. But quit your foolery! Let me attend to putting one foot before the other and you can have your blind man's buff.

A blind man would be steadier on his feet in this darkness.

Be quiet, will you?

Were but an echo to ring out in this mute darkness, were nocturnal birds to sing fearsome, were insects to drone or beasts to howl, were leaves to crackle under serpents' bellies or strange and menacing footsteps to resound, gladly would I be guided by their terrorous noise. But the night passes so still that silence is my dreadful lonely blindness. And you want me to be quiet?

Be quiet, I say!

We'll be lost forever in the night, in this silence, and no trace or memory will be left of us.

Shut your mouth, I say! Quit your sniveling!

Don't be angry . . . Recite me something, won't you?
One of those coplas I like so much.

Be quiet, Diego, by God, be quiet!

Wait! Lo, I think I see something!

Where?

There! Do you see it?

No. What? Where?

There! There!

Where's there?

There! Over there!

I see nothing.

Are you blind?

What do you see?

I don't know . . . Shadows, but lighter; shapes I can't
quite make out . . . Lo! 'Tis people!

What?

Yes, look! People! Travelers lost like us in the dark!

I see no one.

Ferrán! Ferrán! Look! It's the bailiff!

Are you certain?

Hey! Hullo! Over here, don Juan! We're over here!

I see him not.

Dawn is breaking!

What's that?

That dawn is breaking.

What?

Sweet mother!

What is it?

My God! My God!

Diego, talk to me! What in the hell is wrong with you?

'Tis us . . .

What?

I see you over there, and me, and the bailiff.

What are you talking about?

'Tis us, over there.

Quit your foolery, the night is not for joking.

But I swear it!

There's nothing there! There's no one else in this darkness! Can't you see that you can't see? Now see here: that isn't us. 'Tis but illusions, dreams, tricks, traps, chimeras, specters. Hollow, flimsy apparitions. Concocted figments with no more substance than the steam off your humors. The false brood of black bile and phlegm. A composition painted by your consciousness to put something where nothing is because that nothing is beyond conceiving. Hued shadows in the darkness that acts as a black mirror to fantasy . . . Are you listening, Diego? Diego! Say something! Has someone got your tongue? Speak! Are you still there? Diego?

Recital of the Dark Verses

I. Wherein begins the commentary on the "Night," as penned by Fray Juan de la Cruz, commencing with the first line of the first verse which quietly intones "On a pitch-dark night," and which, though quiet, disturbs with its echo or with the clumsiness of its recital a distinct and different night, and the silence of that night or the slumber of its silence.

On a pitch-dark night late in August, or perhaps it was already September, in the year of our Lord 1592, at the most secret hour, precisely as he had been charged by the Royal Justice don Luis de Mercado, and unaccompanied except by his two aides—of whom remains no record or memory beyond the fact that they were two, and who may well have been called Ferrán and Diego as no document survives to refute this—Juan de Medina Zevallos or Ceballos or Zavallos, depending on the source consulted, or even, in certain documents, Francisco de Medina Zeballos, Bailiff of the Royal Court, knocked on the door of the monastery of the Discalced Carmelites in Úbeda.

The prior slumbered. The friars slumbered. Slumbered the brethren, each surrendered to the deep darkness of an imageless sleep. One might say their slumber was but an extension of the poverty, abdication, and austerity of vigil for which the Reformed Carmelites are known, though he who ventured such a claim would be gravely mistaken. On the contrary, they slept as if, having staked all on their souls by day, it was their bodies that triumphed at night. For each slumbered whole in the solitude of his flesh, as only those wanting of spirit may sleep. And they snored. Raucously. Even those friars who delighted in the mortification and privation of their naturals succumbed quite naturally, as if all their flagellations, sackcloth, vigils, and penance had been respired into their flesh through a deep yawn, along with their own selves: tamers devoured by their beasts. Even these snored placidly, their cares and resolve quite unheeded. In his solitary flesh, in his solitary cell, each snored and was joined to his brethren in a chorus of snoring. But in that pitch-dark moment even the snoring had ceased; suspended it hung in the most secret hour. Falling thusly silent, the chorus of sleepers was joined to the silent chorus of their departed brethren at rest beneath burial slabs in the church. The porter, who by rights should be wakeful, had too drifted asleep, with rosary in hand; to judge by the beads passed through his fingers, scarce had he recited the Sorrowful Mysteries when slumber with the monotony of the Pater Noster conspired. When the increasingly insistent, so as not to say thunderous, knockings of the bailiff—who endeavored to reconcile, in a single act, his order to arrive in secrecy and the need to make himself heard in order to arrive—finally awoke the man, more than a waking it was a jolted wrenching from amongst the dead that knew neither hour nor place nor reason, such that not even Lazarus must have suffered greater confusion. Yet that was precisely why the bailiff had come: to disturb the dead. Or so surmised the prior, Fray Francisco Crisóstomo, having been awakened by the recently revived porter, and who, still blind, his eyes crusted with sleep, let himself be led down the cloister and into the chapter house where awaited his unslept and unexpected visitor, all papers and writs and official seals. Such yelling, such orders, such demands. Such threats of excommunication. Such a list of princes and countesses and noblemen and prelates did the bailiff unfurl, among which names the prior managed to recognize only that of the most humble and most honorable and most problematic and most dubious and most tedious and most tiresome Fray Juan de la Cruz.

II. Wherein the aforesaid first line is on that same night followed by a commentary, from the lips of an indiscreet friar, on the second, which reads "by love's yearnings kindled," though its fire be darkened by appetites of a strange nature, whilst Diego wonders in secret if it might not have been better to remain home, far from these shades and excesses.

"It seems the gentle fragrance of our brother Fray Juan has reached the most noble nostrils of Madrid, rousing the appetites of the rich and powerful," said the porter, peeking asudden through the Judas window.

"We know not what you mean, Brother," answered Ferrán, who with Diego awaited the bailiff's orders outside, tempting to countenance both the indiscretion and his surprise.

"That Madrid has sent you to wrench from Úbeda its saint, and from us poor friars the body of our brother."

"We are not permitted to speak," dodged Ferrán, disguising as obedience the insolence of his twenty years.

"Indeed? I had quite a different impression listening to you from the other side of this door," insisted the porter.

"You see?" said Ferrán, seizing the chance to chastise Diego. "I told you to shut your mouth!"

"I said nothing!" Diego, reddening, protested.

"Torment thyselves not," replied the porter, "for in these matters more have I wrought by listening to your master in conversation with the prior."

"Might every doorway prove a university for spies?" Ferrán asked rhetorically, like the student at Salamanca it would have pleased him to be. "I know nary a porter without a Bachelor's in intrigue, if not a Doctorate in loose lips."

"The ear chooseth not its object," rejoined the porter. "Nor does the nose. And mine doth advise me that tonight will not be the night you cross this threshold and set off on your way with the friar's body in tow."

"Speak clearly, Brother."

"I am but a humble porter and know little or nothing of theology and letters. But you do well to speak of the door as a school, for much have I learned in the opening and closing of this one. I know who comes and who goes. I know when and with whom and with what and why. I hold degrees in what happens inside and out, here and there, because this very door is where here and there and inside and out do mix, mingle, touch, swindle, and interlope. I also know that Fray Juan de la Cruz will not cross this threshold tonight. It is not only the rich and powerful of this dark world who wish to snatch that prodigious piece of flesh from the devout of Úbeda. Supernatural forces also have a stake in this dispute. Forces of light and of darkness about which those who sent you, and you yourselves, and even the good townsfolk of Úbeda know naught. Angels and demons quarrel over his bones as if over a soul. But if on some other night you do abscond with the body of the friar, whomever the townsfolk of Úbeda do serve—wretched and ignorant as they are, they know no better than you who their master is, nor whether it is the whip of the soul or that of the flesh before which they cower—they will not let you leave with your quarry; the same rage that blinds them will hone their olfaction and like fearsome dogs will they track you through the night."

"We have taken all necessary cautions," said Diego, swelling from his sixteen years to reach Ferrán's twenty and surpassing them and putting on all the airs of a lord. "In secrecy we arrived and in greater secrecy still shall we depart. Who will tell them, then?"

"Quiet, Diego!"

"What?" countered Diego, once more but a tall and beard-flecked boy.

"Of myself you need not fear. I observe my vow of obedience and the prior has ordered discretion. No one, however, will be able to silence the smell."

"Of what smell do you speak?" asked an intrigued Diego as if he had smelled more than heard these last words, while diligently ignoring Ferrán, whose head was already shaking as it did each time he opened his mouth and to whose disapproval, Diego thought, he should strive to grow accustomed.

"The aromatic clamor of his body. The scent of saintliness. The gentlest of perfumes which stirs in the soul yearnings, burnings, and zeal, and which, emanating from beneath the slab whereunder lies Fray Juan and drifting through the air, at times reaches my own nose like distant jasmine while at this door I stand."

"Is it of a flower's specter, then, that we are to be so afeared?" asked Ferrán, emboldened by the delicacy of his enemy.

"It is of the strange appetites stirred by this scent. I should inform you," the porter said, taking a breath and clearing his throat as one who readies a long oration, "that no sooner had our brother Fray Juan de la Cruz perished than did he begin to exude that most gentle fragrance, though his body was covered by sores. His face grew more beauteous and pacific and less brown and more white and radiant, whereas in life he was rather swarthy of tone. And his dulcet appearance and aforesaid scent inspired among the brethren great veneration. And all arrived on their knees to kiss his hands and feet as if to a holy body they belonged. That scent quickly spread throughout Úbeda like a rumor, waking its people and waking in them unfamiliar yearnings and excesses and making them rise from their beds and wander through the pitch-dark night, for, without knowing how, they knew that Fray Juan de la Cruz had died and they knew they needed to come see him. And come they did, wandering through the night to gather here at the doors of the monastery. And here gathered did they implore and demand entry, but I was not allowed to allow them such. And such were their zeal and yearnings and excesses that I feared they might break down the door or set it alight and thusly I communicated my fear to the prior, who, against all rule and custom, ordered me to let them enter. And enter they did, in droves and, never having been inside and guided only by that scent, they proceeded straight to the cell wherein lay the body of the friar and, though covered it was by infected sores and abscesses, they were roused by the implacable appetite to touch him. And touch him they did. They knelt to kiss his hands and feet and seized the moment to tear loose a lock of hair or at least a few threads from his meager robes. And as the morning arrived, so too did more people arrive. And I opened the door and let them enter. And enter they did, and one after another they kneeled and kissed the feet of the friar. And as my brothers no longer permitted them to tear loose hairs or threads, they entreated me something that had touched his body or been used in his time of illness, and they withdrew contented with the rags used to clean his sores. But when there was not a fiber left of those rags to dispense, the people grew angry and protested and thousandfold grumbled and inquired after the maidens who by custom washed the friar's dressings to discover whether they had any retained. And thus kindled with strange yearnings, the people took to the street. And arriving at the homes of the washmaidens in a clamor they called out to them and in a frenzy they knocked on their doors, and if the washmaidens answered not they made doors of their windows. The maidens were interrogated, or, in the event of their absence, interrogated were their parents or children or any other body who might be inside; interrogated, begged, threatened were their neighbors. The townspeople clamored such that one might say they howled or barked. They smashed locks, forced trunks, breached chests; they searched every vestment and every piece of white fabric did seize. If by chance a wash-maiden had upon her a wound's dressing, if clean they wished it stained with blood and pus and took such a one to be hidden, though in their tireless quest even at the clean ones did they snatch and windmill and amongst themselves did they tussle over each scrap and thread such that I venture had it been gold they would not have pilfered thus. And thus swelled with outrageous furor, with mysterious ardor, with overboiling humors, the people wandered the streets and homes of Úbeda until the bells of the monastery called them to the burial. Persons of all ilk clambered over one another in the church and in the streets to approach and touch or at least see the body. And drunken on that celestial odor arrived the butchers with their knives, and with their daggers the pimps, and the cooks with their skewers, and the blacksmiths with their tongs did arrive. With their saws arrived the carpenters, and with their clippers the seamstresses, and with their needles the noblewomen, and with their razors the barbers did arrive. And the people arrived in uncountable throngs at the ready with blades suited to their office and, standing but notwithstanding their office and standing, all desired the same thing which was their slice of saint. Hairs from the beard, the arms, the

legs to the most discreet. Nails and pieces of ear to the syco-
phants, along with the cracked calluses that had formed on
his feet. But the most daring far overstepped the bounds of
custom. Need was there for the brethren to intervene and
protect the body, as otherwise they would have carved off
such pieces of flesh that when the time came naught would
have been left for us to inhume, or for you to exhume."

"We are grateful for your exhortations, but fear not for
us, Brother. If it is indeed a celestial perfume that endangers
our endeavor, we need only serve a plate of beans to this
ninny," said Ferrán, gesturing toward Diego, "and the wind
he passes along the way shall serve as unmatched disguise,
for, as my own suffering attests, there is a corpse at rot in
that lad's gut and it is far from holy."

III. Wherein, taking advantage of the brief pause and unsound-able void that separates one line from the next, the prior reflects on the agony of Fray Juan de la Cruz, who, though he had been ordered to the Indies, was willed by Providence or Fortune to die in his monastery at Úbeda, a fact which the friar, once installed, well understood, as witnessed in his missive stating that wiser and more timely would it be to make preparations not for the earthly Indies, but for those in heaven, and to provision well for that journey.

Ah, Fray Juan, Fray Juan, Fray Juan. Even dead did he cause trouble, thought the prior. Accursed the hour he came to expire at Úbeda. In rough shape did he come, sick with temperatures and swollen in his right foot, from La Peñuela, where he had awaited dispatchment to the Indies because the superiors of the Order thought him a danger and wished him far. Upon seeing him arrive, did the prior know he would bring troubles, great troubles, immense and innumerable troubles, and he arranged that the friar be lodged in the monastery's meanest cell and treated with great roughness in the hope that such crudity might coax him toward sooner departing. He had never been fond of Fray Juan. The friar's sanctimony rubbed him wrong, and the prior saw his meekness as a form of arrogance. Did he now repent this rough treatment and lack of charity? Who would have thought, thought the prior, that the friar's illness was more than a mere ruse to distract from the serious accusations that over him loomed. Despite the prior's incredulity, the friar's fevers and inflammation worsened and a surgeon extracted an extraordinary volume of pus from his foot. Ulcers and tumors covered his skin and his pain grew ever worse. And it was then that Fray Juan received extreme unction and sent for the fourteen brothers of the monastery. With candelabras in hand, with the De profundis and the Miserere on their lips, did they come, and Fray Juan did beseech them to read from the Song of Songs. "Oh, what delicate flowers!" they say he said upon hearing those verses of love. And they say also that he later said, "Today will I sing my Matins in Heaven." And also do they say that in saying this did he cross his arms over his chest and thusly did he expire in the hours before dawn on the fourteenth of December in the year of our Lord 1591. Who would have thought, thought the prior, that the shriveled creature would turn out to be a saint. Certain brothers of the Order claim to have seen a great light shine forth from the friar's body. Certain brothers of the Order claim that his corpse began to exude a celestial perfume. The prior neither saw nor smelled anything unusual, but he knew that new and still greater troubles would soon arrive.

And arrive they did, one year later, in the form of three men and their mules.

Accursed the hour that Fray Juan got the idea to come die at Úbeda, thought the prior. One of those arduous blessings from which he wished he could free himself. But there was no freeing himself of it, he thought. Even if the bailiff were to disinter the body and transport it to Segovia, performing the great task with which he claimed to have been honored by don Luis de Mercado at the behest of his sister, the very devout and very wealthy and very widowed doña Ana de Peñalosa, Fray Juan de la Cruz would still cause him trouble. Both the brethren of the Order and the townsfolk of Úbeda venerated him greatly and had taken him as a saint and as a saint they wished to worship him, hence one trouble: unauthorized worship was a serious offense and the prior had been admonished by his superiors for permitting it, although nothing had he permitted. But how to halt veneration? According to one brother of the Order, when the time for disciplining came, his arm was stayed by a supernatural force that prevented the yanking necessary for his flagellations, and that the cause of this was none but the fact of his standing on the slab under which lay Fray Juan de la Cruz. The prior believed no such thing, but from that moment on monks and laymen alike refused to set foot on the slab, a condition which carried with it disruptions of movement, distractions during worship, disconcert at ceremonies. Delighted would the prior be to surrender the trouble that was the body of Fray Juan, were that surrender not to occasion new and still greater troubles. He dared not imagine the uproar and grievances that the brothers and the devout might raise upon discovering the body's removal and displacement. He feared, even, an uprising. But of all the troubles had by the prior, this decision was no longer one: the matter was already decided and all that remained to him was to acquiesce and obey. And the idea of obedience was to him sweet and offered respite among his many troubles. And so he obeyed. He acquiesced without complaint and led the bailiff to the church where the cause of all his troubles lay beneath a slab, while the bailiff, consternated by the absence of resistance, went on brandishing ranks, remonstrances, tirades, and letters of marque. Who would have thought, thought the prior, but he could not conclude this thought, for the bailiff with his court of names and his army of arguments, with his papers and his writs, sundered him from his musings to bellow at him new demands. The prior obeyed and ordered the porter to allow the bailiff's aides entry, and to call with all secrecy Fray Mateo del Santísimo Sacramento and Fray Miguel de Jesús to assist in the exhumation. And when they arrived, he bade them be silent. And between them these four did they raise the slab under which lay the body of Fray Juan de la Cruz.

IV. Wherein is recited the third line, which reads "oh wondrous delight!" and is followed by a caesura that is also recited, insofar as Ferrán poses inward an enigma simple and clumsy of appearance but complex of resolution, which to wit goes: "What is yon affliction / which desiring the spiritual / encounters the corporal / and finds therein satisfaction?"

"Such great troubles!" wailed the prior, shielding his eyes as they removed the body, and being first to break the silence that he himself had ordered.

"Such a pain," grunted the bailiff.

"Oh wondrous delight!" cried Fray Mateo.

"A marvel!" seconded Fray Miguel.

Not knowing what they saw or what they ought to be seeing, Ferrán and Diego looked at one another to see whether the other understood. Fray Mateo and Fray Miguel lifted the body and placed it on a table and with the tip of a rod did they strip it of cloth to thusly admire it better. And the body of Fray Juan de la Cruz lay as incorrupt and as fresh as it had upon his death, or at least so the brethren claimed.

"Behold," said Fray Miguel, pointing to the sores on the friar's legs and feet, from which still flowed blood and waters.

"Breathe in, my lords, respire this celestial perfume," said a suddenly inebriated Fray Mateo.

"It is the scent of saintliness!" Fray Miguel concluded as if they had their speech ere rehearsed.

The bailiff smelled nothing, irked as he was. "How will I explain this to don Luis?" he asked himself again and again, temples throbbing angry like a heart betrayed. The prior feared that the scent—which he, being perhaps unworthy of such grace, was not altogether able to olfact—would spread throughout the cloister and wake the brethren, which would mean troubles, troubles, and more troubles. Ferrán found the smell emanating from the body to be, in fact, rather foul, and measured it against the perfumed words of the porter, delighting in their disproof. Diego, however, piled upon the porter's words the elation of the friars and, discovering a taste for the aroma, drew close to better scent it. Brusquely was he pushed aside by the bailiff, who set about examining the body. With the gruffness of a guard handling a recalcitrant prisoner who fainted under the duress of inquisition, he yanked. He tugged at hair and skin. He lifted limbs and let them fall with a thud. Twisted joints. Then did the bailiff amuse himself with the right hand, tempting thence to extract a confession. It was regarding this same hand that the biographers later mused, agreeing that it remained indeed in fine form. Fray Alonso de la Madre de Dios writes: "And thusly observed those who exhumed the hallowed body a unique beauty and alabaster translucence in the three fingers used for holding the quill." And Fray Jerónimo de San José: "Though the body entire remained incorrupt and whole, particularly so were the three fingers of the right hand used for writing, which were so beauteous and white they seemed of purest marble made . . . "

Three fingers of marble like those of a statue.

Three translucid fingers, the alabaster vessel of their writings.

Three verses in flesh.

And the bailiff, drawing swift his knife, did one of them sever.

And it was as though he had cleaved not only the finger but also the tongues of all present, who fell into the translucid verse of silence.

And blood flowed from the finger as if from living flesh. And tongues in mouths did bloom anew.

"A miracle! A marvel! A wonder!" exclaimed Fray Mateo and Fray Miguel, ever more in chorus.

And as if they had previsioned that such a thing would occur, they drew forth from who knows where several cloths for reddening in the miracle that from the wound did flow.

"Clearly," said the bailiff, thrusting forth the friar's finger, "it would be foolish to transport him to Segovia in such a state of freshness."

Ferrán and Diego nodded. The bailiff instructed that the corpse be emptied of viscera and sprinkled with quicklime so it might more speedily dry and desiccate, and that with great secrecy and concealment it be buried once more, for he would return for it in a few months' time. Then he withdrew to see whether the night air might soothe his spirit.

Fray Mateo and Fray Miguel disapproved of the order as an attack on this irrefutable proof of saintliness, but they obeyed, and to watch them gut the corpse, one might even think they savored their labors. More than like surgeons, their prowess in extracting those astoundingly fresh intestines was that of a pair of cooks, for cooks they were in the monastery, while sacristan also was one of the two. Behold the celestial chorizo! And as if already delecting future stuff-meats, gluttonous did they finger the viscous saintliness of the friar's liver, his blessed gallbladder, his gloried pancreas, while Ferrán and Diego tempted to observe not, yet could not but observe, the occurrence.

"At the funeral," recounted a vaguely nostalgic Fray Mateo, holding in his bloody hand that other one, now of four fingers only, "a Dominican friar named Domingo de Sotomayor knelt before Fray Juan and upon kissing this very hand fainted straightaway upon the body. Those of us who observed him prostrate first thought it a veneration, but when we found him unable to rise, to his aid did we rush. The monk later confessed to having concealed a knife in his sleeve and said that as he tempted to cleave himself a finger did he feel the body withdraw its hand, and that such was the cause of his tumult and swoon."

"But another monk," relayed a beaming Fray Miguel, "by name Fray Mínimo, in kneeling before Fray Juan's remains to kiss his feet, took between his teeth the nail of the little toe and sunder did he tear it with a bit of flesh still attached. What a humble man, the others said, and what a suitable name, contented as he was with such a minimal piece of the friar."

V. Regarding the commentary on that line, which, following a break that sundered it from the others like a severed finger, pointed at the "Night" but in so doing pointed at itself, since the line that was a finger was a finger of the author, and of the author did it declare itself synecdoche and news, making it thus an arrow aimed and shot, an arrow speeding toward the ardent heart of doña Ana de Peñalosa, a heart crowned by a tongue of flame, for it is known that aimed at doña Ana was not only the line that was a finger that was an arrow, but also the commentary in prose on those other lines known as the "Flame," penned by the same author: blazing, bracing verses whose blinding light turns them dark despite or perhaps due to the brilliance of their flame and fiery language, which shall later be recited, or not, should the occasion arise.

"What account will I give don Luis of the body? Something something a delicate scent? Something something a supernatural freshness? A supernatural bungle, more like," griped the bailiff on the road back to Madrid. "But by my word, we'll retrace our steps and then trace them again, next time with the friar in tow."

Ferrán and Diego had long ago lost interest in this refrain. What did concern them was whether they would receive their payment due. Given that they returned without the friar, half the agreed sum would be fair. Or some part thereof, at the very least. A little something for the rigors of the journey. But they had not yet aired these concerns with the bailiff, having found, between his rage and his rantings, no chance to do so at any point in their travels.

"Woe is me! What shall I tell the Royal Justice?" the bailiff railed. "That finger had better work the miracle of keeping me in the good graces of don Luis. Wherever my tongue might lack precept or phrase, may the finger serve as my argument. May the finger speak. May it communicate by the freshness of its flesh the impossibility of our venture. May it proclaim the foolery of ferrying the body back only to let it rot along the way. May the part explain the absence of the whole. May doña Ana's appetites be for now satiated by a finger. May the finger keep her entertained while the friar's bones dry and his hide is tanned. May this finger be my tongue and may it amiable speak."

And the finger spoke.

And the explanation satisfied don Luis. And the finger was handed over to doña Ana de Peñalosa and she too was satisfied by the explanation, even as news of the friar's incorruptibility stirred in her even greater desires and urgency. And though firm did she remain in her resolve to recover the body whole, the finger brought her consolation and contentment and served to sate her impatience. Upon this point the biographers agree; it is regarding the finger's ultimate fate that discrepancies abound.

Fray Alonso de la Madre de Dios writes: "On this occasion did they sever the index finger of the Saint's right hand and offer it as a relic to doña Ana de Mercado ... The Lady received the finger and, as I witnessed upon seeing her some sixteen years later, kept it with her always as a precious relic, incorrupt, in a silver box worn always at her breast ... "

Fray Jerónimo de San José writes: "With this departed the Bailiff, bringing as consolation for the Royal Justice and his sister, and as testament that the body was not yet ready for transport, the finger severed therefrom, which was delivered by the hand of Padre Fray Juan Evangelista into those of the King's Confessor, Fray Diego de Yepes, and by his hand into those of His Majesty Felipe II, in whose power and great veneration it remained."

But a finger would not satisfy doña Ana, no matter how translucid and incorrupt, no matter how beautiful as a poem. The noblewoman suffered from the same yearnings and zeal as the townsfolk of Úbeda, though unlike the townsfolk of Úbeda this zeal and these yearnings were not new to her or unfamiliar: she had her own excesses years earlier foreseen when first she met Fray Juan de la Cruz. And likewise unlike the townsfolk of Úbeda, she would not be contented with threads or rags or dressings; unlike Fray Mínimo, she would not be pacified by a toenail. Nor would she be pacified by that beautiful verse of alabaster flesh she treasured between the flesh of her breasts. She desired the body entire. And the body entire would she have. Not because her appetite was greater than any other's, but because she could. Beyond being wealthy, beyond being the sister of a Royal Justice, doña Ana was also intelligent and prudent and timely cautions had she taken. To the gold escudos Fray Juan de la Cruz needed for his monastery at Segovia had she had tied a clause that, die where he might, the friar's remains would rest therein. And now, with the aid of her brother, she would see this clause executed and duly enacted. Much did doña Ana and don Luis struggle and many efforts did they expend and many postponements and delays did they weather in royal palaces, in archiepiscopal palaces, in squalid monasteries. Many a coin did roll and much ink was spilled, many hands did they kiss in obtaining from Padre Fray Nicolás de Jesús María, Vicar General of the Discalced Carmelites, who at first had so recalcitrant been, license to transport the body from Úbeda to Segovia and an order of excommunication should the prior at Úbeda refuse to relinquish the body to the bearer of these missives.

The body entire: such was doña Ana's will and desire and perhaps the will and desire of Fray Juan, as well. She liked to think so, at least. After all, it was to her that the friar had dedicated the explication in prose of "Love's Living Flame." After all, it was to her that one of the last letters Fray Juan de la Cruz had managed to write in the throes of his illness had been addressed. After all, it was to her that Fray Juan de la Cruz had said, on their final visit, that she ought not feel sad because to her he would return. And return to her he would. She, Ana de Mercado y Peñalosa, had turned that perhaps offhanded remark into a prophecy, and the eight or nine months that had passed while they tempted to pacify her with a missive made of flesh seemed to her time sufficient for the drying and hardening of the body, and to her it seemed high time to fulfill, in one fell swoop, both prophecy and clause. Yes, return to her he would, she said, and kissed the friar's finger. And she sent for her brother, and her brother sent for the bailiff, and the bailiff sent for Diego and Ferrán, and Diego and Ferrán and the bailiff set out for Úbeda once more.

VI. Wherein the night of the first verse is revisited in order to better expound it, and it is revealed that the lines "Oh wondrous delight!" and "for my house had gone quiet" are repeated in the second verse or strophe or night, though in chanting the same is the same made different.

Night, again. Úbeda, again. Again the monastery doors. Again the bailiff's cries waking the porter. And again the porter waking the prior and again the prior receiving the bailiff. No, false: the prior was gone from the monastery that night. On this occasion was the bailiff received by the subprior, Fray Fernando de la Madre de Dios, and it was to him were handed the missives and writs. And while certain biographers claim that it was Fray Juan de la Madre de Dios and Fray Pedro de San José, let us nonetheless imagine it was Fray Mateo and Fray Miguel who, together with Ferrán and Diego, raised once more the slab under which lay Fray Juan de la Cruz. Where there is accord is with regard to the date: the twenty-eighth of April in the year of our Lord 1593.

Though the cast be uncertain, the roles were unchanged from the prior occasion and each player knew his lines and likewise how the scene would end: with the body of Fray

Juan de la Cruz hidden in a trunk on the back of a mule. Even the corpse behaved as expected: though its flesh was not yet fully consumed, the quicklime had done its work and they found the body drier and more cadaverous. According to the friars, it retained its delicate scent. But resignation had supplanted surprise.

They will set out at the hour most secret, following the bailiff's plan; they will choose deserts and solitudes over busier thoroughfares, that they might evade their foes. They will travel at night, that they might avoid the putrefaction, flies, and worms which the sun's heat might inflict on whatever in that body remained soft and moist. And only at night, moreover, though the bailiff voiced this not, for the dark had long served thieves as cloak and shield, and thieves indeed they were: holy thieves, as certain poets might come to call them, or vile thieves, thieves for hire, thieves serving a law that always favors the rich and powerful, as the townsfolk of Úbeda will certainly describe them upon discovering their theft.

Though several hours remained before dawn, they needed make haste if they meant to reap the benefits of the dark and gain advantage over their foes. Yet while the bailiff was exhorting Ferrán and Diego to hurry the body into its disguise were they by unexpected footfall and shoutings on the other side of the church door interrupted. At the top of his lungs, an unforeseen friar demanded entry. Entry was he denied, but the subprior stepped out to calm him. It was Fray Bartolomé de San Basileo, who claimed to have seen the angel of the city of Úbeda appear before him in fierce struggle against the angel of Segovia. He said that a great voice had spoken to him through his slumber and had woken him up with the words: "Rise, for they are taking the body of the saintly Fray Juan de la Cruz." The subprior ordered his silence and ordered him back to his cell and ordered him to remain there in prayer until the subprior himself went to fetch him. And Fray Bartolomé, who had tended to Fray Juan in the last throes of his illness and who had grown of him quite fond, obeyed, against his will and his wishes he obeyed, but it was too late: improvisation was once again possible and hope had supplanted resignation.

None could say whether it was the delicate fragrance that stirred a sudden appetite, or whether the same voice that had stirred Fray Bartolomé from his slumber did breathe the idea in the subprior's ear, or whether it had been gestating gradually, carefully, cautiously all these months in the mind of the prior, who then entrusted it to the subprior before departing should the bailiff return in his absence, and it was only by the irruption of Fray Bartolomé that the subprior's daring its moment did find; what is certain is that, as the bailiff exhorted Ferrán and Diego anew to hurry the body into the trunk, they were interrupted by a new and unexpected condition from the lips of Fray Fernando: that the body of Fray Juan must be divided, one half thereof to remain in Úbeda.

Great was the bailiff's bewilderment. And on the heels of his bewilderment swift followed ire and the familiar litany of orders, excommunications, writs, threats, permissions. But the subprior stood firm. Certain was he that a piece of the body would be better than its absence entire, and that, once the exhumation and translation was made known, such a piece might placate furies and soothe souls and channel devotions. Likewise certain was the bailiff of the need to negotiate in haste lest more shouting wake more visionary friars or the townsfolk of Úbeda and lest the dawn surprise them with its light, stock-still in their obstinacy.

A *not half the body but a leg* was met by a *not a leg nor a hand but an arm, but not that arm for its missing finger*, followed by a *but that is the whole point,* and a *throw in three toes and two fingers, then,* an *absolutely not*, a *no*; thusly and so on did the subprior and bailiff argue without reaching an accord. Nor could the saint's biographers agree: Jerónimo de San José claims that one of his legs was severed to remain as consolation at the monastery in Úbeda, while José de Velasco notes, "The monks did sever one arm to keep with them a token of whom they so loved." We could, of course, retreat from polemical anatomical assertions and state merely that the monks severed a limb, for the subprior would settle for no less and the bailiff would concede no more, but, being numerous the accounts by fortunate pilgrims who claim to have seen in the monastery of San Miguel at Úbeda Fray Juan's arm safekept in a striking case of silver, we shall say it was an arm.

VII. Wherein is recited, in full and in order by the good Fray Mateo, each verse of the "Night," and are the general qualities of these verses expounded, while also discussed, upon Ferrán's urging, are several dark particulars of that wondrous night.

"Madre Teresa erred not when she said those little bones would make miracles," said Fray Miguel.

Ah, Teresa, the true fount and motor of all this commotion. Teresa Sánchez de Cepeda y Ahumada, the daughter and granddaughter of conversos whose name conceals an Esther and who did fiercely condemn her youthful addiction to chivalric tales, but who found in reforming the Carmelites her purpose, and in her fervor to restore its traditional ways did she find windmills upon which to loose her own knights-errant, and her quill found ink, and her prose material abundant. Many years earlier had Teresa de Jesús met in Medina the young friar who was then Fray Juan de Santo Matía but had ere been Juan de Yepes and who, though he did not yet know it, would soon be Fray Juan de la Cruz, the first Discalced Carmelite, back when, disillusioned as he was by the laxity of the Order, he was eager to abandon it for the Carthusians. But needing holy gents to found the first monastery of the Discalced, Teresa saw what mattered in that priest so young and serious and, so what, so small. "Though he be little, I know him great in the eyes of God," wrote Teresa in 1568, no sooner had she met him.

"Her exact words: little bones. Not bones. Little bones," explained Fray Mateo.

"Madre Teresa always got a giggle out of Fray Juan's modest stature," Fray Miguel went on, "and indeed was he slight, as you yourselves have seen. 'Here comes a friar and a half!' our founder was wont to joke upon seeing Fray Juan approach in the company of one of our brethren."

"Fray Juan did not find this amusing, but he found humor in few things indeed," explained Fray Miguel. "He was not one for jokes, unlike our Madre Teresa."

Slight though it was, great pains had the friar's body caused the men in their efforts to fit it into the trunk, even after its mutilation. They had also wrapped in cloth and carefully safekept the arm which the Discalced of Úbeda would keep as consolation. The subprior and the bailiff were off composing the clause that would account for their new accord and signing documents of receipt. Meanwhile did the friars improvise for Ferrán and Diego a dinner or breakfast, depending on one's perspective, of garbanzos, asparagus, and sundry leftovers, that they might not take to the road on an empty stomach, though perchance this hospitality was merely an attempt to delay their departure.

"Scarce half a friar was he, and now without the limb we trimmed is he even less," sighed Fray Mateo.

"Such a delicate burden shall bless the flanks of your mules!" exclaimed one of the two friars, who were increasingly hard to tell apart.

"Such diaphanous cargo!" exclaimed the other.

"A bird soon to take wing!" exclaimed one. "And like the branch beneath the bird, my heart is by his departure stirred," added the other.

"How dearly shall we miss him!" they concluded in unison.

"Delicious asparagus!" exclaimed Ferrán, tempting to shift the conversation, weary as he was of so much Fray Juan this and Fray Juan that.

"Asparagus?" asked Fray Miguel, slow to understand. "Ah, yes . . . Fray Juan enjoyed asparagus, as well . . . "

"One of the very last foods he craved," explained Fray Mateo.

"It was a miracle indeed to find them so far out of season," reminisced Fray Miguel. "But God wished to bestow on his servant this gift of flavor."

"Already was he very ill," Fray Mateo explained, "and only with the greatest effort could he swallow . . . "

As if the dead friar himself had regurgitated it, Ferrán let fall the asparagus he had been raising to his mouth. Diego, meanwhile, seemed to find fresh seasoning in the anecdote and repasted with renewed gusto.

"His great pains scarce left room for hunger," explained Fray Miguel.

"But great hungers did his anguished flesh and the

prodigious substance that flowed from his ulcers inspire," remembered Fray Mateo. "One of our brethren," Fray Miguel went on in the remembrance of Fray Mateo's memory, "chanced upon a bowl o'erbrimming with this pus. Given its sweet fragrance, he took it for a tasty pottage and consumed it entire . . . "

Ferrán felt his stomach turn. He felt nausea. He felt a retching.

"Entire!" squealed Fray Mateo.

Another retching, this time more intense. Diego looked at him perplexed.

"Entire!" squealed Fray Miguel. "And he ate it without revulsion, but indeed with great gusto, as he himself later attested."

"You see no possible excess in your devotions toward a man not yet enshrined?" Ferrán finally vomited.

"He shall be, my child. He shall be," replied Fray Miguel. "The countless miracles Our Lord has performed since his death to his saintliness do attest."

"Though also in life was he famed as a saint," explained Fray Mateo.

"And well known was his skill at exorcising demons," continued Fray Miguel.

"And several nuns claim to have seen him levitate in the throes of prayer or upon receiving the Eucharist," added Fray Mateo.

"And his verse . . . " managed Fray Miguel before he was interrupted by his own elation.

"Ah, his verse! Such celestial coplas did he compose," finished Fray Mateo.

"Coplas count neither as miracles nor as proof of saintliness!" Ferrán rejoined.

"These do," replied one of the friars. "I assure you, my child, it is as if they were dictated by God himself: so divine is their craftsmanship, so elevated their depth."

"How extraordinary their music!" exclaimed one, turning their colloquy into a tournament of praise.

"How harmonic their inflections!" ventured the other.

"How their doctrine trills!" advanced more forcefully one of the two.

"A lesson in love the likes of which you never heard!" triumphed the other.

Whereupon Fray Mateo rose with candle in hand and, adopting manners, postures, and gestures less reproachable in an actor than in a Discalced Carmelite, began to recite with great affectation:

On a pitch-dark night,
by love's yearnings kindled
—oh wondrous delight!—
I slipped out unminded
for my house had gone quiet.

In darkness, without fright,
down hidden stair I snuck

—oh wondrous delight!—
in darkness, with fine luck,
for my house had gone quiet.

Out into that wondrous night
I stepped unseen and stealthy,
with not a thing in my sight
nor any light to guide me
but one burning in me bright.

That lone flame did guide me
surer than the midday sun
to a place where awaited he
who could be no other one,
and where no one could I see.

Oh night! You that guided,
night kinder than the dawn!
Oh night! You that united
Beloved with his lover yon;
a lover into her Beloved transformed!

Soft upon my flowering breast,
which I kept for him alone,
his slumbering head he lay to rest,
and as my fingers traced its crown
a breeze did spread the cedar's zest.

From the turret a zephyr fanned,
as his fine locks I stroked,
when with his ever placid hand
he left a wound upon my throat
and all my senses did he suspend.

With cheek pressed to the Beloved
did I stay, and myself forget;
all ceased and I ceded,
leaving earthly worriment
among the lilies quite unheeded.

Fray Miguel and Diego erupted in cheers and applause. Ferrán, for his part, applauded only enough to avoid accusations of bad manners but not so much as to leave any doubt as to his discontent.

"What say you, good sir?" asked Fray Mateo of Ferrán, flecks of affect still clinging to gesture and voice.

"I know not . . . "

"You know not what?"

"I know not . . . I know not. The coplas are not bad, but neither are they good. They are . . . strange."

"And how are they strange, my child?" asked Fray Mateo, adopting anew the role of friar.

"Fray Juan speaks with the tongue of a woman," blurted Ferrán. "Moreover—and I beg pardon should this strike thee as coarse—in this voice does he moan as a woman with a man. Which would not be so bad if . . . "

"'Tis the sound of a soul delecting in God thou hearest in that darkness . . . "

"Why bring God into these coplas?" rejoined Ferrán. "Nowhere in the poem is He mentioned."

"Art thou not, perchance, familiar with the great King Solomon's Song of Songs?" Fray Miguel managed to interject.

"I am not and know not and trust not . . . "

"It is hardly strange that they should be strange to you," countered Fray Mateo with the patience of an aged confessor. "The strangeness of both miracle and verse appeals not to our comprehension but rather to our capacity for wonder . . . "

"And quit likening poems to miracles!" thundered Ferrán. "These coplas move me less to wonder than to mistrust. Verses deceitful as a woman and, worse still, voices misleading like those women who wander the night and later, denuded, prove to be the counterfeit concealment of men. Mark that he himself . . . in that feminine guise, taking advantage of the dark . . . how brazenly . . . "

"Lo, thou hast understood nothing," interrupted a weary Fray Mateo.

"Ere have you set foot on the road, already are you lost," judged Fray Miguel. "But we trust that while finding your way in the night you will stumble upon the truth of these verses."

"Silence!" the subprior shouted quietly upon entering the kitchen, if such a thing were possible; rather, gesturing a shout he shouted without shouting, emulating great volume in great quiet. "What hubbub is this? Numbskulls, do you wish to wake the brethren? And you: ready your mounts, your master waits impatient. You must set out in all haste, for the hour most secret draws nigh."

VIII. Wherein, still sheltered by the night of the first verse, having not yet left it behind but with entry swift becoming exit, expounded are its last two lines, which read, "I slipped out unminded / for my house had gone quiet," and—dogged task—an attempt is made to commentate the abyssal silence that rifts this verse from the next.

On a pitch-dark night, at the most secret hour and the minute most still, when astral bodies spin not in the heavens nor do the clouds that cloak them advance, when in the depths of the well is the moon's light extinguished and silent falls the cricket, when nary a floorboard creaks nor an ember crackles nor does any lamp sputter its last, when water ventures not a droplet nor the wind a rustling leaf nor the tree a fallen fruit, when lovers entwined remain but form two separate slumbers as distant one to the other as to a stranger asleep, when the near-born calf is not and the newborn child cries not and the near-dead man neither dies nor stirs nor coughs nor recovers yet finds momentary quarter in that moment when even Death labors not, when both flea and mosquito halt their torment of the unsleeping and, swollen with blood, rest contented beside a bare ceded back, between one verse and the next, between one moment and the next, when time is suspension and by the hand of the clock does one second become a minute and one shaftment a league, at that hour most secret, from the monastery of San Miguel at Úbeda, before the blank stare of the porter, with the body of Fray Juan de la Cruz hidden in a trunk and lighting neither torch nor candle nor lantern to better travel dressed as shadows in the shadow of night, in stealth and silence and in great haste did depart—or in great haste did depart not but rather were departing, or rather in their extended departing did they stand stupefied as if something had detained them in the fixity of that instant—the bailiff, Ferrán, and Diego for a different night or a verse darker still.

IX. Wherein the verses of the "Night" unfurl segments of a narrow solitary road which great labors and fatigue and darkness do promise, but also, the bailiff and Ferrán and Diego wish to believe, many honors and daybreaks and great fortune, and thusly is expounded the tenebrous fourth line of the poem's third verse, which reads "nor any light to guide me."

They departed. With the body of Fray Juan disguised as luggage. From the Discalced monastery of San Miguel they departed. From the city of Úbeda they departed. And in darkness and in secret did they take to the road.

Up front rode the bailiff on his mule, followed by another mule bearing the trunk, and following that mule were Ferrán and Diego, also mule-borne.

The solemnity of their silence, the gravity of their countenance, the rigor of their darkness: in tempting to hide the deceased did they ever more announce him. All who saw them would glean in those shadowy travelers a funeral procession whose paschal candle had burnt its last.

But how alive they were. How crisp the air in their nostrils. How jolly their fear.

Behind its inky facade, the road did content them and

spurred their impatience for the adventures it promised. Ready as their blades they rode.

Alert as beasts through the barren night they rode.

In silence they rode.

Or nearly.

"Ferrán," whispered Diego, tempting to evade the bailiff's ear.

But Ferrán preferred to ignore him. He was keen not on words but on combat and clanging irons and flesh wounds. If the bailiff had ordered them silent, it was not merely to avoid giving signal to possible pursuers, but also that they might hear their foes from afar whenever they might approach. And with intent and expectant ear did Ferrán hear them arrive not.

"Ferrán," Diego insisted.

Such a vex. Such a vex, that Diego, and such a vex the tardiness of that promised foe who arrived not, who complied not, who appeared not for the appointment announced months prior by that charlatan porter.

And their pursuers did not that night beset them, nor did they the following night appear. Mayhap because the bailiff, in caution and to better foil their foe, had elected to abandon the camino real to Madrid and detour instead toward Jaén and Martos, or thus ran Ferrán's justifications upon passing Jaén. Would they come? The next night? Because this night, considering the distance traveled, could offer but a few moments more of darkness, from which the bailiff seemed intent on wringing every advantage ere the light of dawn forced them to seek refuge. The dawn, as ever near and ever promised as the enemy, and like the enemy seeming ever more distant and unlikely, for the darkness along this detour did ever thicker and denser grow.

What trees were those that lined the road? Trees or rocks were they? And rocks those shadowy forms? A hill, that mass of darkness yon?

"Halt!" thundered a voice from parts where no one stood.

And as if born of supernatural throat did that voice inspire in them great admiration and plentiful dread, and the hairs stood erect on the heads of Diego and Ferrán, and on the head of the bailiff so erect did they stand that they raised the hat from his brow, and the hairs on their bodies, which were many, stood erect and man and beast halted obedient, and immobile did they remain in elongated terror. But fore the following terror they dared, at least, to bare their weapons and scour with their eyes the darkness, though no one did they see. And, not knowing at whom or toward where, the three men surrounded the trunk and aimed in all directions.

"Who goes there?" ventured the bailiff.

"Who lieth there?" replied the formless voice.

"Come forth and show thyself. Who speaks thus?" demanded the bailiff, wresting aplomb from his freight and his age and his faith and his arquebus.

"One who, unlike thou, knoweth who thou art, O villainous grave-robbing sacristan. Whereto takest thou the body of the saint? Leave it whither wast!"

And thusly was the bailiff convinced that he who spoke formless in the dark was the dark itself, the night made flesh, the prince of darkness.

"O Demon, bar not our path but return to the inferno from whence thou hast emerged," said the bailiff, making the sign of the cross with his weapon as if he planned to discharge a Christ.

"Clotpole! Thou wouldst better heed thine own advice and retire whence thou camest. What knowest thou of night? Of the dark? If for the Devil thou takest me, then to the Devil listen well: know that the night thou seekest to cross two forms of darkness doth sow. The first is bitter and horrific to the senses while the second hath no peer, for it is dreadsome and terrifying to the soul. Retreat. Let not thy resolve to hold fast the flesh of the saint be thine own undoing. Return to Úbeda. Return the body to its tomb. For in proceeding wilt thou enter a darkness wherein will serve neither lantern nor taper nor torch. Only the flame that within thee burns bright may serve thee as guide. Though, as the Devil well knoweth, the light of all stars and fires and flashes combined beguiles not like that emitted by the heart of man. Yet even so, when thou art plunged into that pitch-dark night wilt thou wish to tear out thine own heart and hold it before thine eyes. And tear it out thou shalt, only to discover by its fleeting flare that the footfall thou didst hear, the foe tracking thee in the dark, was naught but thy heart's own beating. Thou hast been warned. Let it not be said that the Devil offered thee no words of caution in the night, if only to correct the silence of God."

No sooner was this oration ended but the birds began riotous to announce the dawn.

The first rays of sun displayed the men disheveled and sweatsoaked and ridiculous, still aiming their weapons at they knew not what. They laughed upon seeing themselves so. In relief, in shame, in mockery, in continued befuddlement, they laughed. And they lowered their guard. They had survived the night and triumphed over no one.

"Let us make haste to find haven and shade to protect the body of the saint," said the bailiff, "lest the sun's light bring a ruin that the Devil's darkness could not."

And astride their mules did they resume their journey, or rather did they make a detour from their journey in the direction of a nearby copse, or rather did they make a detour from their detour in the vicinity of Martos, fleeing from a light more fearsome than the dark.

X. Wherein Ferrán, keen to rush ahead of his companions on the dark and secret road of the poem, that is, in his hurried arrival at the second line of the fourth verse, which reads "surer than the midday sun," is returned to the last line of the prior verse, whose music and image give rise to the other and which reads "but one burning in me bright," and thusly does Ferrán participate in the advance and retreat which is the nature of verse and which distinguishes it from prose and which derives from the Latin versura, *in olden days what peasants called the turning of the plow at the end of one furrow to begin the next, and in this returning does the verse illuminate for Ferrán an image that had earlier been hidden from him by the hastiness of prose.*

"Ferrán," called Diego to the one who traveled beside him.

But Ferrán was spun in his thoughts. The previous night occupied him like a dream returned to mind the next day by the slightest trifle only to depart again, leaving distance and disquiet in its place. And so as he progressed did he regress. It had not been the combat he'd awaited, no. There had been neither blows nor wounds nor show of skills, but rather mere words pronounced by a foe who had caught them off guard when most they expected him.

An enemy both supernatural and unlikely, for, once both befuddlement and night had passed, and unlike the bailiff, Ferrán was loath to call him a demon. He had noted in the affair echoes of the amphitheater, of passion plays, of inspirational liturgies, above all in that voice which reminded him ... of whom? Of whom, of whom.

"Ferrán."

The sun did high in the heavens shine when asudden he understood: Fray Bartolomé de San Basileo! Yes! The voice which had in the dark spoken thus was that of Fray Bartolomé! It must have been. Fray Bartolomé, who had tempted to keep them from taking the body with claims of an angelic parley, of a voice that had roused him from slumber to his mission. Yes! It was he, it was he, it was he who, diligent, did disobey the prior's orders and follow them through the night to revive his act of supernatural ventriloquism. Always is it thus: man usurping the labors of God or the Devil. What the devil cared the Devil, if he did exist, whether or not the body of Fray Juan remained in Úbeda. Yes, it had to be, it was Fray Bartolomé—there was neither doubt nor demon about the matter. Clearer he saw it than the midday sun. Once the black curtain of night had been raised, the scaffolding of that devilish dispute exposed it as a one-act farce. And thus satisfied did Ferrán tower proud over Fray Bartolomé de las Comedias and over the bailiff and Diego, who now seemed to him like sucklings afeared of voices cast in the dark.

"Ferrán!"

A dark voice froze him on the verge of announcing his triumph. "Silence, Ferrán," it warned, spewing its black spittle. And but one drop of this dark spattering was all it took to turn all Ferrán's bluster to shadow. Afeared was he, this time with no trace of joy, that if he unmasked the man disguised as the dark whom the bailiff took for the Devil, unmasked too would be the bailiff, who, wounded by his lack of surety, vulnerable for his supposition, humiliated by the childishness of his ferocious faith, would, in revenge, accuse him, Ferrán, of being a heretic or a Moor or a Lutheran or a Judaizer. Countless men and women filled the dungeons of the Holy Inquisition for less, he feared.

And fear he did.

And his fear began to spread.

And that drop of darkness began to spread and to shroud reason and words and arguments like ink spilt. And when its blackness overtook all, terror blazed in the dark.

In the middle of town, his grandfather was burning at the stake.

"Marrano! Marrano!" shouted the throng.

Fervent, blinding, ferocious, insatiable light.

"Ferrán," insisted Diego.

"Quiet!" barked Ferrán, not at Diego but at the little boy who wailed as he watched the flames rise.

XI. Wherein upon Diego's request does Ferrán offer a commentary on the fifth verse of the "Night," although, as if unwittingly obeying the note in which Fray Juan de la Cruz himself advises that, while his verses "must be commentated somehow, one need not be bound by their commentary," in attempting to give it plain does Ferrán unbind its lines from their figures, comparisons, and similes, and thus unbound and loosed in all their mystery do these rise, oh nocturnal shimmers, oh pitch-dark flares, into the morning bright.

"Ferrán."

"What?"

"Nothing."

"Nothing?" chided Ferrán. "You have hounded me all this way to say nothing?"

They had stopped to rest in the shade of a great tree. Among its roots had they found a hollow wherein to lodge the trunk containing the friar, which they covered with leaves to better protect it from the swelter and from unforeseen eyes. And the bailiff offered his aides some of the wine he kept for himself, in celebration of his great exploit and victory over the Devil. And he repeated without end that what had passed was proof of the deep ire harbored by the

Prince of Darkness over the great devotions that awaited Fray Juan de la Cruz in Segovia, and of his powerlessness in the presence of such a relic, for neither to show himself nor approach had he dared.

"With this chunk of saint we carry, no devil can stop us, nor any hex need we fear!"

Diego nodded with canine enthusiasm. Ferrán bit his tongue.

The revelry was followed by wine-smelling yawns. Then the bailiff offered a reminder that they would take turns so one might sleep while the other two stood guard, himself being the first to rest.

"Ferrán."

"What?"

"Only that . . . well, that I did not understand what you said about the verses of the friar moaning like a woman does with a man," ventured Diego, finally.

"Ah, that! What, have you never been with a woman?"

"Of course! Many!"

"Had you been with but one, you would know them straightaway."

"What?"

"The moans," said Ferrán. Before continuing, he made certain the bailiff slept. Indeed, he snored. "Listen: Oh night something something."

"Oh wondrous night," corrected Diego.

"What?"

"The line goes, Oh wondrous night!"

"I know that, you dunce! But it matters not what the line says. Pay the words no mind. What matters is not what the poem says, but rather what it moans. Mark how the saint's verse crumbles into amorous whimpers. Listen:

Oh night, something something!
Oh night, something else!
Oh night, I know not
who is what nor who is who
with whom, or not, nor who is who in whom!

An "Oh!" escaped Diego's lips.

"Oh, yes. The poem entire is naught but a holy rogering: it begins with amorous yearnings—and oh what yearning, what burning, what fever precedes that bit of fondling, oh such fondling, and then the friar earns his sausage: oh, oh, oh. I'm coming, the Coming, I came. Then the final verses round it all out with yawns and snuggles and post-coital caresses. A rogering, quite Aristotelian in its rising action, climax, and resolution, though dissolution might be a more fitting term for these couplets . . . "

"So you believe not that the verses were dictated by God as the brothers proclaim?"

"I haven't the foggiest. But tell me this: how could a friar know such details? Perhaps these verses should be taken as proof not of sainthood, but rather of a laxation of vows or perhaps even sodomy . . . "

"Sodomy!" exclaimed Diego, blushing. "Do you think

... Do you think the friar ... Do you think that is why the Devil appeared last night to claim his body?"

"I say only that if eager are we to liken verses to miracles, I have heard miracles finer and fuller pass the lips of young men in taverns: miracles perfectly crafted to the opening of windows and balcony doors—and far worthier of praise than those which relieve the malarias and pleurisies and toothaches of devout crones and merit no more marveling than the commendation offered a village barber—for truly great a feat is it to enter the chambers of a handsome maid, safeguarded as they tend to be. These verses serve young lovers better than any ladder, though there is need of a ladder, as well, for the miracle to be performed as befits. I myself have composed a verse of love or two in my time, to prodigious effect, though not one of those ladies, relieved of their nocturnal affliction, ventured indiscreet the next morning to call me a saint or announce any miracle."

"Have you composed many?"

"A few," replied Ferrán, winking an eye and barely concealing the puff of his poet's chest. "Let us say that I, too, have turned a phrase ... and that my verse has served me amorously on several occasions. Such is the nature of coplas. The fevers that drive them are spent before the effect of their rhymes and meter."

"Sing me one!"

"No."

XII. Wherein, while the bailiff and Ferrán and Diego wend their way through the night, diverse nights or verses are into one single night or verse muddled and on that recited muddled night are recited and expounded, to even greater muddlement, the first two lines of the first verse of verses diverse from the "Night" but of selfsame shadows and dark substance made, known as the "Spiritual Canticle of the Soul and the Bridegroom Christ" or the "Spiritual Canticle" or, more briefly and belovedly, the "Canticle."

Darkness.

Were Fray Juan de la Cruz to open his eyes asudden, what would he see? Darkness. And since awakening from his mortal slumber never would he think himself packed in a trunk like three doublets, for how absurd a thought, would he then in his confinement imagine himself in the depths of a tomb? Or having been returned to the nightmare of his cramped prison at Toledo? Perhaps. Were it not for the footfall of the mules announcing their gradual transit along the camino real toward Toledo. Toledo? Already were they on the road to Toledo? At what dark hour did they arrive unseen at Córdoba and unseen leave Córdoba behind? Had they passed first through Baena like shadows under the light of the moon? Had they stopped at a shabby guest house for pilgrims in Castro del Río? Had they reached Ciudad Real? Not yet? Are they near? How many days would it take them? How many nights had passed? How could they tell? The darkness has been filtering in through the dreams of the bailiff, of Ferrán, and of Diego, tenebrous dreams that occupy hours through which the day normally spins, overflowing their banks and blending different nights into one single continuous night.

Darkness.

Why have they halted? Who is speaking out there? Of what do they speak? Darkness: darkness is what the bailiff should tell those who ask what he bears in his trunk. A darkness most dark. Those noisome guards would have fled in terror. But gruff, surly, short on foresight and long on lawyerings, he responds with threats and cautions. He trots out the same old bulls, orders, and letters patent that authorize him to pass all duty and checkpoints without making register of his cargo. The men argue and Ferrán readies his weapon. As do the guards. And a few words and coins thereafter, they resume their journey at mule-pace.

Darkness.

Blindfolded at night did they bring him to Toledo. At the height of the war between Calced and Discalced did the Calced detain Fray Juan on the charge of grave insubordination. In Ávila did they detain and flagellate him "to see whether by toppling that column of the Carmelite reform, the whole structure might crumble," as one biographer will later phrase it. And to Toledo did they bring him in great secret. At night did they bring him. Blindfolded and round-about did they bring him, that he might not know whereto. To Toledo? Are they headed for Toledo? And in their efforts to shatter his resolve, that he might renounce his barefoot-edness, was he found guilty of defiance and contempt and sentenced to prison for as long as the Order's leadership deemed fit. Then did they cast him into a cell with other prisoners, and later into a different cell that was darker and well nigh as cramped as the trunk, that greater might his suf-fering be. And suffer he did in his captivity from December 1577 until the middle of August 1578, in a cell "which barely fit him, diminutive though he was," Teresa de Jesús will later say, failing to hide a faint smile behind her distress.

Darkness.

How could such a small space hold so deep a darkness, whoever might open the trunk would likely ask. How could such a small body hold so many a torment, Teresa must have asked. How could the flesh endure so many pains, pri-vations, humiliations, whippings, worms, fleas, fasts, crusts, sores, stenches, dysenteries, degradations, disciplinings, iso-lations, sleepless nights, fevers, chills, ulcers, wounds, and all that darkness, the hagiographers would later ask, rhetor-ical, delighted. But those external afflictions and darknesses did pale beside those within, the friar himself will reply: "a deep and profound darkness; the soul feels itself to be per-ishing and melting away in the presence and sight of its mis-eries, in a cruel spiritual death, as if it had been swallowed by a beast and felt itself being devoured in the darkness of its belly . . . " The friar pressed deeper and deeper into that pitch-dark night of the soul and into the abyss of his spirit did he descend. At times he thought he would die, at times he wished he would die, and a thousand times did he die and dying was he when one day or night—in that endless night it was hard to know one from the other—one day that was for him the same eternal night, from inside his dark and cramped prison he heard somewhere in the distance, in the street, out there in the strange world of the living, a young lad pass by singing a villancico:

For you I die of love, my sweet. What am I to do?
Then die indeed you must, good sir, forsooth.

A young lad passed by, singing the friar's pain. And what passed by was life itself. It was life, singing of death. And death was just a song of love sung idly by a young lad. And love was a young lad passing by. A young lad singing, who into the darkness vanished.

Darkness most dark.

And in the darkness, somewhere in the distance, crossing the night, from the past, there on the road did and does Ferrán sing a silly little ditty. He recites his amorous braggartries, which the bailiff tolerates and Diego admires, and which cheer all three and amuse their travels. Naught have they heard from the townsfolk of Úbeda and so mayhap none follow in pursuit: May it please God our Father and the good Virgin Mary, trusts the bailiff, amen, and forsaking caution and care does he begin to hum along. And timidly hums Diego asoft as he feels the lines pulse within him as if loves of his own they were. And over and over does Fray Juan hum the villancico that, wounding him with love, has restored him to life. And he begins to stammer other verses, different ones and darker still, for hearing that ditty has roused him to write verses of the night, which he composes in his memory in the hope he might transcribe them later if by chance he should procure ink and paper or by charity these should be procured for him by a new jailer. And thusly does he begin to compose his "Canticle." Thusly does he transform his solitude and forsaking into heptasyllables and hendecasyllables of affliction, and from both does a whimper or sigh escape the confines of their meter:

> *Where have you hidden,*
> *my Beloved, and left me moaning?*

Darkness.

And so stammering liras, phrasing sighs, wording breezes, humming dawns, hushing musics, stuttering loves, confecting darkness and luminosity, does Fray Juan delight and amuse himself in his tenebrous confinement. And with each verse he writes does the night of the page grow darker and more impenetrable. While among the biographers there is no agreement as to whether the verses of the "Night" were also composed in this prison or after his escape, those nights belong not to any before or after but rather to that same night of his escape: escape from sense, escape from speech, escape from self. Coplas in which the friar "uses as a metaphor the wretched state of captivity, from which it is a wondrous delight to be released," as he himself explains in a text that, multiplying the confusion among nights, he will also call the Night.

Darkness most dark.

The night of the prison, the night of the soul, the night of the poem, the night of the ink, the night of the poem's recital, the night of the escape. Oh paper most black! Oh palimpsest of nights! And Ferrán and Diego and the bailiff sing their way along the long dark road that does or did pass, or will perhaps pass again through Toledo, crossing the illuminated night or the night of the illuminated page.

XIII. Wherein Diego is offered by his dreams a commentary on the third line of the first verse of the "Canticle," which reads "like a stag you fled, after leaving your wound," and this figure or image of the stag appears before him, wandering fugitive through a shadowy forest, only to escape its representation forthwith, leaving Diego to dream the absence of the stag and the dissolution of his own image in the dark bestirred waters of the dream of no one.

"By chance, good Sirs, what bear ye in that trunk that so delicate an odor emits?" inquired the innkeeper, ecstatic.

Ah, the delicate scent! The celestial aroma! The friar's holy odor, of which neither the bailiff nor Ferrán nor Diego had ever caught whiff despite abundant notices and which, even should they ere have gleaned it, they now assumed lost amid the vigor of their own salubrious and virile fragrance of road, dust, leather, and sweat cultivated over many days and many mules.

"Nothing that would warrant such indiscretion," reproached the bailiff.

And the innkeeper did wrinkle her nose as warning that they would not be so easily rid of her olfaction. They had passed Ciudad Real and were nearing Malagón when at daybreak they stumbled upon the inn. They had known not how fatigued they were until the proximity of a bed loosed the reins of their exhaustion. The bailiff had paid the inn- keeper a fine sum that they might be lodged at a remove and beds were prepared in a storehouse near the stables, but while they brought their luggage inside had the innkeeper grown drunk on the aroma. Now the bailiff's words had to her inebriation and curiosity added offense, and offense and inebriation and curiosity were joined and multiplied as one by one did the woman's daughters arrive. First timidly and then brazenly did they arrive. Abandoning their labors, kindled with strange yearnings and convened by the aroma did the innkeep's five daughters, who more than daughters seemed five ages of the same woman, begin to appear.

"Waft it in, my girls! Waft it in! What smell ye?" goaded the innkeeper, and now the noses sniffing out an answer were six.

Beset by ayes and sighs and queries did the three men tempt in vain to rid their lodgings of innkeeps. No sooner would Ferrán remove one from the trunk upon which she had pounced, another would take to the pouncing. And in the bailiff and Ferrán's inability to best this enemy, whose combat required weapons unfamiliar to them, did Diego sense that his moment to shine had finally arrived.

"They are perfumes!" ventured the lad, thinking this might quench their curiosity.

"Perfumes?" repeated insulted, unsatisfied, incredu- lous one of the nuisances.

"Perfumes and liniments," offered the lad, tempting to compensate his insufficient response by elocuting like a fairground peddler. "Balms transported from the Orient . . . "

The bailiff's hand flew to his brow. Ferrán shook his head. All was lost.

"From the Orient! I knew it!" cried the youngest innkeeper, acting the eldest.

"Rose water, I'd wager. No, no, wait . . . Essence of jasmine and orange blossom!" ventured the mother innkeep.

"Amber!" mooned another.

"Of course not, pignut! 'Tis civet!" railed yet another, as if for a gallant suitor they vied.

"'Tis amber!" the daydreamer insisted.

"Have you ever smelled amber?"

"Once did I dream its scent, and it was just like this . . . Amber . . . "

"'Tis not amber, but musk," yet another joined the competition.

"Amber . . . "

"No, you dimwits. 'Tis elixia."

"Elixia? What is elixia?"

"Suffice it to say the mystery of its name is fine matched to its scent."

"What knows this numbskull of Oriental aromas?"

"You tell me, you garlic-chewing pumpion!" assailed her rival.

"Hush, liar! Your lips reek of sulphur from all the falsehoods you spew!"

"Open the trunk and show us the fragrant jewels it holds," ordered the mother innkeep.

"That our eyes may feast on that which now delights our noses."

"From the flowers and rosebushes wafts the scent of amber . . . " incanted the daydreamer, bewitched.

"Permit us at least the perfume's colors. Our looking will do their aroma no harm."

"Alas, a deaf ear must I turn to your entreaties," apologized Diego, who knew not how to get out of this mess, "for hard penalized would be any violation of this lock, the sole key to which is held by doña Ana de Peñalosa, a great Lady who impatient awaits in Madrid these caprices of her vanity."

"A great Lady? A Duchess? Is she very fair, this doña Ana?"

"Some trace of noble beauty still abides in her haggard face," Ferrán interjected, brandishing the weapon of his elegance in an attempt to remedy the situation, "yet despite her riches, poor rival would she be to your zest and beauty."

"Leave thy honeyed words and let us come to numbers. Name your price. Inflate no more our yearnings as fine well shall we gather the sum amongst us."

"Break not thy money box in exchange for disappointment, here shall ye find naught but tinctures, ceruse, carmine, and blubber: vile prostheses for dishonest faces. Leave the purgations to the sick and the bloodlettings to the dying, for even the dearest medicines might turn the healthy ill. These artificious unguents are the sad luxuries of age and homeliness, though they offer no cure. Consider this: What half-wit would light a lantern under the midday sun? Tell me: What fool would bedeck with silk flowers a meadow in full bloom?"

"Permit at least our noses their delight and stand not between us and those delicate airs."

"Stand ye not between our weariness and its relief but allow us the rest for which we have so handsome paid," countered the bailiff, leaping back into the fray.

And with much shoving and cajoling did they manage to eject from their room the innkeepers, who though sweetened by the gallantry of Ferrán intractable remained, and forthwith did they barricade the door and entrench themselves within.

"A fine mess that tongue of yours has brought us!" chastised the bailiff while Ferrán tempted to shoo the innkeepers from the small window through which they took turns peeking.

"Never shall we rid ourselves of these crack-brains now! Worse yet, with the name of our patroness did you regale them, selling cheap our route. Little shall it cost our pursuers to learn it. The friar's body will not rest safe here, for the blade has not been forged that can slow a woman in pursuit of a frivolity. And since it was you who sketched in their desire the perfumes by which they will from innocent oglers into sagacious thieves be transformed, it shall be you who stays awake and you who stands watch and you who guards the trunk with your life while we recover the strength that will so crucial be if we are to leave this place."

And Diego obeyed. In spite of his weariness did he stand watch. In spite of his hunger. In spite of his melancholy. But was this strange melancholy melancholy indeed? Oft returned the innkeepers with false offers of this service or that message, but Diego let the snoring of the bailiff and Ferrán answer their calls. He heard an ear take post against the door. He saw an eye peek through the keyhole. A nose poke through a crack. Flowing locks grow long from the bald tile roof. And every fissure in the wall became the lips of a monstrous mask and through those lips did the innkeepers laugh and sigh. Diego was wracked by shudders of breast, throat, tongue, teeth, lips. And discern could he not whether it was fear the innkeeps inspired in him, or yearning. Was this desire a desire for diversions with those women? What to name this morose passion? How to baptize this ice akindled? Was it fever? Thirst? Was it exhaustion? It was the scent of the friar, concluded Diego. The celestial odor that kindled yearnings and excesses and had so intoxicated the innkeeps and so stirred his own self. Yes, it must be the scent, though smell it he could not. Yes, the body of the friar must be the source of these errant appetites: the external marrow, gland, or mysterious organ from which those humors secreted that, perfuming the air with their seed, did bestir whomever breathed them. Diego looked at the bailiff, who reminded him of his father asleep, and wounded was he by longing. Then he looked at Ferrán and was wounded by a longing sharper still, though he knew not to what or whose memory that longing belonged. But was it a memory? Was it longing? Diego yawned and weariness arrived like a house gone quiet. And the snores and the sighs and the snickers did slowly lull him to sleep.

He was roused by a swift kick to the rump from the bailiff, which rescued him from the penance of the dark dreams wherein his spirit thrashed.

"Scoundrel! You confuse snoring with waking, sleeping with watching, dreaming with guarding! If only you could shut your mouth so well as you shut your eyes! Were you not my wife's nephew gladly would I hand you over to those madwomen, for you have served them far better than you serve us. Yet this is not the time for justice," he continued more gently, "but rather for escape. Quit staring at me like a stag at a hunter and get to your feet."

Night was falling. At the bailiff's sign, Ferrán swung the door inward, bringing with it two or three innkeeps. He tempted to usher them toward the patio, from whence he then called for the others.

"Come hither, dear ladies. Hear me well, for my words are to you of great concern. Tell me, have you by chance heard account of the nuptials of Thetis and Peleus?"

The women's bewilderment would no greater have been had Ferrán speechified in Aramaic or pressed a lemon to their lips after promising sweet Medjools.

"Hear this, dear ladies, for once upon a jovial and nonexistent time in the days before time, in that time so distant from our days but so near to our nights, a mortal king was to a sea nymph wed. Now, at the celebration arose a peculiar contest over a golden apple inscribed with the words *For the fairest* and three goddesses did in this pageant compete: Hera, Athena, and Aphrodite. Of this impossible deliberation did they name a mortal as judge. Hear this, dear ladies, for much have we deliberated, my companions and myself, and still we rack our brains, because your desires are our own and though boundless is our desire to bestow upon each a perfume, meager is our means. Thus have we concluded that but one bottle can we subtract without injury to our patroness or evidence of thievery and punishment for such. May said bottle serve as golden apple and prize for the fairest among ye. Oh nymphs of Judaea!"

"Nymphs of Judaea?" the mother innkeep echoed wary. "Of whom do you speak? Be it known that here are we all good Christians."

"Please forgive, dear ladies, the daring conceit that clumsily tempted to convey in one breath the maritime airs of gentile mythology and the austerity found in the Testament of the Prophets, which are by your pulchritude united. So equal are you in beauty, and in Christian virtue so evenly matched, that hard won will be the competition we propose. How to judge the beauty of a rose: in bud, in blossom, or in full bloom? Or in any of its rich and varied intermediaries? Quite the contest, and twofold harder to judge than the one amongst the goddesses, their being three and your being six and six moreover of the selfsame beauty, what twofold, the task is sixfold impossible! Now hasten to your abodes and spruce as if for a wedding: drape yourselves in your finest gowns, braid flowers and sprigs into your locks. And then return bearing carafes of good wine, that the battle of beauties might be waged and your loveliness illuminate this dark time, albeit briefly, as in that blissful Golden Age."

Thirsting for perfume, kindled with yearnings, possessed by strange passions and to comeliness aspiring, beguiled by promises, flustered by cryptic words, liberated to their sisterly rivalries, and, finding not at all disagreeable the judges who as mirrors to their vanity would serve, the innkeeps accepted the terms of the competition. Heeding Ferrán, to their abodes did they hasten and amid laughter, insults, and sighs did they spruce as best they could, now accomplices, now enemies, dressing one another's locks and donning their paltry gowns; one even produced a ribbon that she had for some improbable occasion safeguarded. Oh nymphs of Malagón! But when they sought their reflection, gone was their mirror: they knocked for the judges and the door opened not. They called out and the men answered not. They peeked through window and grate and saw no one. They forced the door and inside they found no one. Only the vanishing trace of perfume.

XIV. Wherein resounds a mute echo of the song of Philomela, the ill-fated princess who, after being savagely raped by her brother-in-law Tereus, King of Thrace, and after having her tongue severed by his sword to sunder her call and clamor for justice, contrives to spin a poem, embroider a page, weave a text begging for aid which she sends to her sister Procne, who with the aid of Dionysus rescues the wretched girl, and together they render bloody vengeance upon Tereus, after which the two are transformed, one into a lark and the other into a nightingale, as observed by Ovid and other heathen authorities, and from this transformation follows the nightingale's song and, it follows, every poem, for Philomela means "she who loves song" and that song is a canto is a verse is a wound is her mutilated tongue is the song invoked in the second line of the thirty-ninth verse of the "Canticle," which reads "the sweet nightingale's song," for this nightingale is none but Philomela, whose foreshortened tongue communicates in silence with the friar Juan de la Cruz, himself short of tongue before a plenitude he cannot convey in words that fall short, phrases that fall flat, concepts that feel narrow, and yet even lacking thus his tongue does he persist in transforming through his verses, like Philomela in the form of a nightingale, the impossibility of speech into song.

The night was cold and the stars, ice. And colder it grew as they wound their way up the knoll. Afeared that the inn-keepers would alert the townsfolk of Úbeda to their where-abouts and destination, the bailiff decided to twist their course once more; the detour, however, proved more for-midable than their foe. A long, steep, grueling, vexing, dark journey had they made when in the distance they glimpsed a fire like yearning ablaze. Though they drew not their weap-ons, the three men raised their guard. When they reached the source of that resplendence, however, they found but a few carefree shepherds warming their hands. And yet, had they learned anything from their visit to the inn, it was that unforeseen dangers might anywhere lie hidden. Innocent adversaries, for example, were the flocks of sheep that barred their passage with their slumber. The shepherd in charge, a lad slightly older than the rest, who answered to the name Fabio, approached them.

"May God keep you good gentlemen," he said in greet-ing. "Have you lost your way in the night?"

"If this dark road leads to Toledo, then lost our way have we not," the bailiff replied, wielding his tongue like a sword swung through brushwood.

"Some do say this road leads to Toledo," the shepherd rejoined. "But also have I heard that few arrive, and that there are safer and more central paths. Not many travel-ers dare venture these far-flung roads, and not one of them at night. Have you good gentlemen not been warned that these hills are ensorcelled?"

"We have no fear of sorcery: God our Father and the Virgin Mary protect and bless our journey."

"And who says, good gentlemen, that Providence did not place us shepherds along your path to keep you from danger? Come, come, warm your hands by the fire and rest a while, for at dawn do dark spells lose their force and the shades that wander this forest return to their caves and dens. No sooner have the birds announced the morn, and before the first ray melts the ice that now glitters in the heavens, will we spread across the hills to graze our flocks, and you good gentlemen may with greater surety continue on your way."

A beautiful shepherdess smiled at the bailiff from the glow of the burning timber. True it was that the episode at the inn begged a heightened sense of mistrust, prudence, caution. Yet also true was it that the shepherds seemed neither to have noticed their luggage nor smelled any perfume emanating therefrom. And that they had traveled much and eaten little, and that it was not long until the dawn, and that they would sooner or later need to find a place to rest and it was not as though a couple of fireside hours spent avoiding the cold would mean arriving two hours late to the sepulcher. And so to the surprise of Ferrán and Diego did the bailiff accept the shepherd's invitation, though he relieved not the mules of their blessed cargo when he tied them to a tree, should they later have need to depart in haste.

The shepherds shared their rustic meal—cheese made from sheep's milk with bread, olives, grapes, and

pomegranates of rich sweetness—and the travelers, voracious, gave thanks. Wine flowed freely and abundant. And
quickly, too quickly, were kindled conversation and laughter and music from flutes and smoldering glances between
shepherdesses and travelers. Cold had given way to fever.
But was wine the sole flame behind this burning, or was the
wine itself enflamed by a supernatural force that rendered
more sultry and savory its combustions? Was it the body of
the friar that caused these accelerations? Was it the Devil?
Was it the dark spirits of the forest that danced thus amongst
the flames? For even the bailiff, so unwaveringly dour and
restrained, did join in the dance, and even Diego, whose lot
it was to blunder with maidens, chatted lively with a plump,
pleasant tender of flock. Phillida, a young shepherdess dark
of complexion and of charms well endowed, held fast the
gaze of Ferrán, who, to impress her eyes and delight her ears,
alleging gratitude for the hospitality of their new friends,
readied himself with great flourish to recite a few coplas.

There was, among the shepherds, a maiden they called
Philomela. She was young, handsome, and mute, and she
wore a coarse deerskin over her white woolen clothes. Her
locks were golden, her eyes dark, and murky and confus-
ing was her life story as told by the plump shepherdess
to Diego, who, from her parade of indiscretions, intrigue,
names, rumors, betrayals, lies, secrets, messages, proverbs,
communications, circumlocutions, statements, revenge,
justice, songs, and silencings, from her gory eclogue did
manage to glean that the lord of those woods, accusing her

of calumny or heresy or witchcraft, had ordered his sentries to cut out her tongue in order to punish her crime and free her from the danger of a future sin. When Ferrán finished his coplas, Phillida adorned his brow with an improvised crown of ivy as befits a poet. And among the hurrahs and wine-sparked applause, Fabio approached Philomela, who, sensing his intentions, did tempt to slip away but was stayed by Fabio's fast grip on her hair.

"Now shall we hear the song of sweet Philomela," Fabio announced.

And with shouts and jostlings did he force the young shepherdess toward the center of the huddle of pastors and travelers as if his insistent hospitality had sprung only from his desire to display her. Pale, trembling, shame-faced, a monster exposed, a thing to be seen, captive in the cage of a crowd that did savagely demand her impossible song, the mute was mute twice over.

She raised a hand to cover modest her mouth but upon a savage gesture from Fabio she obediently opened her fingers like lips and then opened her lips and then withdrew her hand. Not a sound could she make, but Philomela stretched wider and wider her tongueless mouth and still from that abyss did no sound emerge. Instead, she seemed to inhale all sound, for as she opened her mouth all music and noise and voices ceased, as if her absent tongue were the eye of a cyclone of silence that in its whirling hushed all that was nigh. Such was the sweet, painful, terrifying song that Philomela sang and did not sing.

Motionless, dazed, amazed, delighted, flabber-
gasted, dumbfounded, Diego. Bloodred trickled the juice
of a pomegranate from the corners of his mouth as if in a
spasm of emulation, a mute mimicry, a carnal echo, he had
devoured his own tongue. The fruit remained in his hand,
as close to his breast as the Christ in Diego's town church
did hold his heart, inspiring in him the same rapt incom-
prehension. Trampled at his feet bled another pomegranate, the basket having been overturned in rough carousal.

And though no sound did she emit, the silence began
to slip off key with the painful spasms of Philomela's futile
exertions. Then she belched bloodcurdling an amorphous
mass of sound. Not a voice, but the ghost of a voice that
bemoaned the long-lost words that gave it meaning. At
times a heartrending, disjointed, spectral wail, at times a
cacophonous echo, a ghastly arrhythmic hiccough, the mis-
carried facsimile of a primitive utterance, the clamorous
failure of a phrase attempted, a simian moan.

The crowd applauded to hurry her silence, but
Philomela persisted in her song. Satisfied, Fabio rushed her
curtsy and pulled her aside and with a wave of his hand the
flutes struck up again with redoubled fervor. And merry
was made anew, as suited the youth of the shepherds and
the wine and perhaps also the body of the saint. And too
was the dance rejoined, conjoining couples in its mad spin-
ning and disjoining them to join others while still others
were in Love's wheel spun.

Diego looked at Ferrán, who, with dancing gait and

Phillida's hand in his, slipped ever nearer the shadows. He looked at Philomela, set apart from the others with lips still parted: he wanted to kiss her, he wanted to fall mute in her mouth, he wanted Ferrán to see him in that kiss. But Ferrán was occupied in another kiss when Diego kissed Philomela, when Philomela acquiesced and Diego's tongue probed curious the absence of Philomela's, and once more was there in that shadowy cavern, that dark den, that formerly empty oyster, a tongue.

And all asudden did the shell clamp shut. Philomela's teeth seized between them Diego's tongue, now nearly hers, now bleeding. And Diego's cries fell mute within that deaf mouth. Unspeakable pain was never better said, or, better, not said. Nor could he call for help, his tongue being in another's mouth; in vain did he struggle to decouple himself from the shepherdess. And so it was that in order to rid himself of Philomela, Diego needed to rid himself of himself: to rid himself of Philomela he needed to rid himself of his tongue and thereby become Philomela, himself. And the pain grew unbearable and Diego's mind went dark and his surroundings turned black and he felt himself fade, and yet in this blackness he believed he heard a voice or the ghost of a voice sing or hum or whisper, wordless, "Oh night! You that united Beloved with his lover yon." What he heard not was the shrieking laughter of Ferrán and the bailiff, nor did he suffer their ridicule and mockery or see Fabio squeeze his arms around Philomela's waistline in a violent embrace, forcing her once again to open her mouth.

XV. Wherein naught occurs nor is any verse expounded but rather is kept, mute, a secret.

The clumsy portrait of a young Dionysus painted by an apprentice in the style of his mediocre master: thus appeared Ferrán snoring in his inebriation, his crown of ivy askew but fast upon his head, sprawled across the grass of the morning after, surrounded by grapes loosed in the orgy.

A short ways off, wounded by music, vanquished by dance, sacrificed to their own excesses, dead to themselves and the world, did lie the bailiff and Diego with wine stains on their shirts that resembled, or perhaps indeed were, blood.

The dream had awoken before the dreamers, for on the knoll of those nocturnal shepherds not a ewe remained. The Bacchae had moved on to other pastures. Only the mules still tied to a tree gazed upon the vomit-flecked scene from the remove of their beastly beatitude. Meanwhile, hidden from view, forgotten inside his inner cellar or trunk, upon the body of Fray Juan de la Cruz was being sketched a darker, more mysterious Dionysus: one maimed and mutilated, of flesh divided and devoured.

Dionysus the twice-born. Dionysus who stirs strange

yearnings and follies and excesses and who with wine and song and dance whips all souls into a frenzy and incites women to maim and men to dress as women. Dionysus, that effeminate god, rested close by.

XVI. Wherein the bailiff shines his torch upon a blind man and, in so doing, unwittingly renders them both a dark allegory inscribed with the words "may my eyes behold you / for you are their light," lines from the "Canticle" which are here expounded, though not in their full breadth.

Footsteps, laughter, murmurs.

For many leagues now had the three men wandered lost after the bailiff decided to abandon their detour and press into the wilds, seeking errant their way back to the camino real. And though lost all knew themselves to be, none dared say as much: the bailiff, to protect his pride; Ferrán, to avoid contradicting the bailiff; and Diego, to avoid moving his tongue, which sore and injured did remain after that silencing kiss.

And, lighting no flame to avoid giving any sign, they stumbled. In darkness and in silence did stumble man and mule. Blindly and knowing not whereto, but pretending to know or knowing not that they knew not, they stumbled. And as they pressed further into the wilds of their own silence did their hearing grow sharper and soon could they discern footfall on dry leaves, breaths, laughter, murmurs.

The bailiff halted, as if by clearer hearing might he better trace the form of those sounds. Could the townsfolk of Úbeda be upon them at last? But the sound in their pursuit had stopped with them and the bailiff heard naught, nor aught did Ferrán and Diego hear.

No sooner had they resumed their errant march than did Diego stumble over a stone. And tumbling from its own height did the stone begin to roll in an infinite descent toward itself, rounding around its empty center as it rolled. And the stone did reach its center. And the stone did disappear. And again were they stumbling when those footsteps, those murmurs, that breathing, and that crunch of leaves resumed behind or before or around them, nearly stepping upon their steps or at least so it sounded. Was it Dionysus on the back of a panther with his entourage of Bacchae, satyrs, and fauns? Was it the innkeepers turned by trickery into vengeful maenads who, still bedecked in their finery, thirsting for perfume and drunk with rage, stalked them thus? Could it be the jocund shepherds playing a prank on them for a few more laughs? Again did they halt and again halted their spine-tingling company, as if they were by their own steps followed.

Could it be the footfall of their own fears? Taking their insistence on darkness more as hindrance than prudence, the bailiff lit a torch. But by its flame was no one lit. No one, save the mules and the three ashen men.

"Who goes there?" thundered the bailiff.

But no one answered him. Could it be the shades that wandered those woods?

"Well do I know you fear not to unsheath your swords; indeed, to that I know you eager," the bailiff told his aides, "just as I would gladly cast myself into a bloody brawl in defense of this sacred mission that has unto us been entrusted. Yet I hold that this be a night of marvels and terrors during which little will serve iron and fire, for the enemies that stalk us are of matter more diffuse than flesh and of nature more like shadow. It is they who have confused our course with their dark arts. Prudence dictates that we find refuge wherein to pass this terrorful night, by preference a chapel or monastery or some sacred place. May God our Lord and the Blessed Virgin Mary protect us in this dark hour."

"In the name of God our Lord and the Blessed Virgin Mary, have mercy on this blind admirer and tell him if by chance you have upon his beloved lain eyes," said a stranger who appeared out of nowhere.

Ere had the man said his piece, already did they for a fearsome enemy take him. And fearsome indeed was he: long of hair and beard, unclothed, filthy, forsaken. What they could not divine was whether he was supernatural or human of nature. Ferrán awaited not the verdict and instead drew his knife on the stranger, who reacted not.

"Who are you, and where are your companions hidden? What are you after?" inquested Ferrán, who took the man to be from Úbeda come.

"This lone admirer seeks only his beloved. Tell me, good sirs, have you by chance seen him?"

"Your beloved? Might this beloved of yours by chance be a corpse?" insisted Ferrán.

"Tell us," interjected the bailiff, "what manner of thing are you?"

"Tell yourselves, good sirs, if eyes ye have yet in your heads, for this admirer lost his own staring into those of his beloved in the waters of a crystalline fount."

"A fool, a dimwit, a nuisance, a madman! That is what you are!" the bailiff cut him short.

"Or a man who feigns madness," mistrusted Ferrán.

"Might he not be one of those hermits addled of brain by lengthy penance in the desert?"

"More likely one of those beggars who wander from village to village catching charity by surprise ere the novelty of their misery be spent."

"Or an alumbrado who hid from the gaze of the Church in these woods only to be struck by a ray of divine justice."

"Or a fugitive from the law, for his dismal pallor, nakedness, and sores may be taken as signs of recent captivity."

"To the labors of your gaze does this blind admirer offer himself, as the icon does to he that hews it, that paints it, that gilds it."

This, then, was a man—strange though he was, no doubt could there be that he was human of nature—a man small and dark of complexion, of indiscernible age behind his ample beard, and of dubious blindness, for neither did his eyes suggest darkness nor did his hands grip a staff. He wore naught but a few tatters tied round his waist that managed not to cover his sizable misery, from which Diego managed not to avert his eyes. The docility of this alleged blind man offered at that dark hour a taste of order and control, and his ravings did distract them from their errancy.

"Well? Which does best match your person?" the bailiff insisted. "Tell us, which art thou?"

"My beloved once said, I saw my lord with the eye of my heart. I asked him: Who art thou? and he answered: Thou."

"And wherefore wanders a blind man, if blind truly you are, through the night?"

"What the blind admirer does in daylight so too does he in the dark: he begs for sights. Good sirs, by your mercy, have you not seen my beloved pass through these woods?"

"We have seen no one."

"Then indeed have you seen him, for my beloved's beauty is like that of no one."

"No one have we seen, but we have heard footsteps, murmurs, laughter. Do you know to whom they belong?"

"This poor admirer did indeed hear those sounds but when nearer he drew to them it was you good sirs he found."

"Do you know the road to Toledo?"

"This poor admirer does not."

"Do you know of a monastery nearby?" asked Ferrán.

"This wounded admirer does not."

"Or how to reach the nearest village or estate?" asked the bailiff.

"This solitary admirer knows not."

"What do you know, then?"

"This blind admirer knows only a sight most secret, a love sketched on the heart of the lover: those eyes most desired, which the admirer wears tattooed inside him and in the dark of his insides do open and see."

What wind, what breeze, what gust did snuff the torch asudden?

Darkness.

Darkest darkness.

And in the darkness resounded anew the footsteps, breaths, laughter, murmurs.

And in the darkness two eyes do open and see.

And in the darkness does Fray Juan see a line of lighter shadow form: the sliver of a door ajar. The guard must have left it thus, a mercy or a negligence or a miracle. Or had the friar himself loosed the screws from the lock? He will from his dark and cramped cell escape, thinks he, dizzy with hope.

The door leads to a hall and the hall to a vast arcade and in the arcade a window that overlooks a small landing on the city wall below, and beyond that the rocky cliffs that lines the river Tagus. Tying strips of sheets and blankets together he fashions a rope that, though long, will fall short. It matters not. He will escape. Into the pitch-dark night will he escape, bringing with him his black papers, his pages smudged with shadow, his nocturnal notebook illuminated with verse. He ties his rope to a hook. He removes his habit and casts it into the night. And down the hidden stair of his verse climbs the naked Fray Juan de la Cruz as far as his tongue allows him and then he leaps, into the night does he leap, into the unspeakable, into the vast.

He falls.

He flies.

He vanishes.

Into the "Night" did Fray Juan vanish, for what is that poem but an escape: a flight from the self, a flight from sense, from speech: a few amorous words fading into orgasmic moans, a linguistic spasm into which the poet vanishes and no one appears.

When the bailiff managed to relight the torch, it was an absence he illumined: the trunk with the friar's body was gone.

Shock! Stupor! Fear!

Gone too was the stranger, that mad or blind or sembling admirer, just like the stone upon reaching its center.

XVII. Wherein, in commentating the third line of the first verse of the "Canticle," which reads "like a stag you fled," does the verse manifest in Diego's vigil as the image of a dream he'd earlier dreamt and which was earlier recounted, and the next two lines and a few others besides are likewise commentated, but, these verses being so secret and of such swelled and surfeit sense, do they from their commentary flee like the stag in flight, and from the comprehension of Ferrán and the bailiff do they escape, and only scarcely and in darkness do they to their glossing acquiesce.

Diego ran directionless through the dark. After their initial bewilderment had Ferrán ventured a theory that veered from the bailiff's supernatural explications: the sembling blind man had been naught but the guile of the townsfolk of Úbeda, who, no sooner had he blown out the torch as a signal, arrived under cover of darkness and stole off with the body they believed to be theirs.

"They cannot have gone far. Hurry! Let us part ways to cover more distance and pause not until he is found!" ordered the bailiff. "Make haste, now. Run!"

And Diego ran along wavering routes, for discern could he not where to direct his steps. He knew neither where to look nor what to do should he find, since amid all the hurry and stupor the bailiff had no further directives given. Face those many men all alone? Stalk them in silence? Depart to alert his companions, at the risk of losing their foe? But were he to find the friar's body, were it he who salvaged their endeavor, then would his missteps be set right in the eyes of the bailiff and would he gain, perhaps, the admiration of Ferrán.

A sudden stag emerged from the darkness. A great stag in great haste. A stag beautiful under pale starlight as the veil of clouds briefly lifted. And Diego thought it to be much like the stag of his dream and after his dream did he run. Diego ran after his dream because he was young and foolish, with little experience of the world or knowledge of life or dreams and their dangers, deceptions, and stalkings. Forgetting all care and logic, Diego ran after his dream because his dream, at least, traced a path where none had been. Diego ran after the stag as if the stag were Fray Juan de la Cruz fleeing in the pitch-dark night after stealing his own body. Diego ran after Fray Juan de la Cruz as if Fray Juan de la Cruz were a thief who had stolen his dream. And he ran after his dream and after the thief of his dream and he ran after the stag like a stag as his heart pounded in his breast. And nearly had stag set upon stag when he was lost. In the darkness was he lost. And yet it was not the stag that was lost, but Diego. In the darkness did Diego find himself lost. He knew not where he was and he knew that he knew naught and he feared that if he went on, he would no longer know even who he was. But go on he did, and already knew he not who he was. Diego had left Diego behind, crying in the darkness like a terrified child. But on he went, he went on through the darkness neither like the son of man nor like the son of stags, he went on knowing not who he was, he went on and was no one.

And no one was there when the bailiff passed by.

And when Ferrán passed by there was no one. Or rather he saw no one. But there where no one appeared he heard what appeared to be something and paused as not to scare off those sounds with the sound of his steps. They were whimpers, and he thought of Diego. He thought perhaps Diego lay wounded having happened upon the townsfolk of Úbeda. But whimpers were they not: they were laughter. But laughter were they not: they were tears. But tears were they not: they were moans.

And from the darkness did emerge a pair of eyes. Dull and pale and blind like the eyes of a statue but rounder and more agog as if from their hollows had they been released. But eyes were they not, he gleaned, they were nipples followed by a huge, handsome pair of tits. And also did emerge, in the pale starlight as the veil of clouds briefly lifted, an arm, a neck, the soft curve of a belly, the waist of a beauty denuded and dismembered like a statue emerging from antiquity, and a mouth.

"Ferrán!" Ferrán heard Diego call to him from the abyss of that mouth he recognized as Philomela's even before the face of the shepherdess emerged full from the darkness.

"Ferrán!" called that tongueless mouth as if it bore borrowed or stolen Diego's tongue. But it was neither the tongue of absent Diego nor the absent tongue of Philomela that spoke to him thus, it was his own. And Ferrán attended to the call of his own flesh which from that other flesh did speak. Ferrán, kindled with strange yearnings as if driven not by the call of his own body but rather by that of the friar, drew near to Philomela and drew Philomela to him. He tempted to kiss her, or to find Diego's tongue with his own in those abyssal depths, but Philomela withdrew her lips and disdainful did she turn her head. Then did Ferrán hear laughter, Philomela's dreadful laughter, yet it was not Philomela who laughed thus but Fabio, who was in the darkness like a hunter lurking. The shepherd stepped nude from his hiding place, where likely he had been reveling in Philomela before Ferrán passed by, approached them, and, all laughing and taunts, did wrap them both in an embrace. Ferrán gleaned that into a trap had he fallen, but, kindled with yearnings of love, he resisted not when the four-handed hermaphrodite stripped him of his garments.

For Ferrán did want to lose himself in that sweet assault. He wanted to lose the lost body of the friar and he wanted to lose his own body in those other two, and he wanted in that losing to save himself from the terrorous night. Ferrán wanted to lose himself in that wide-kneed taking but did not want to be taken on his knees. And Ferrán began to lose himself in that wanting and not wanting. And amid myriad ticklings and titillations and tendernesses did Ferrán lose himself in that back and forth of wantings. In that gambol of hips did Ferrán lose himself in that heaving of backs. In that skyward pitch of his lance. In that mute colloquy of soft and stiff. In that swelled arrow aimed straight at him. In that sweet struggle between she and he wherein he was suddenly so she. In that she. In this that did Ferrán lose himself, so other again and so outside himself and suddenly so inside and so himself. And in that inside himself did Ferrán lose himself in not discerning his self from theirs. In not knowing whose cock, whose cunt, whose hole was whose did Ferrán lose his body in the pitch-dark night just as Fray Juan had lost his own. And in being three they were also none and those spread legs did to no one belong.

No one.

No one was there when Diego, or he who had once been Diego, or the stag that was no longer Diego, passed or did not pass by.

No one was there when the bailiff passed by. He saw no one. He heard no one. And stealthy he stalked through the darkness to where no one could be seen. Where are you hiding? wondered the bailiff of Fray Juan's body like a hunter wonders of his escaped prey. And like a hunter did he sharpen his senses in search of a trace in the dark. But the sorry gloss of a hunter must he have been, for he failed to notice the true hunter who, emerging from the shadows in the pale starlight as the veil of clouds briefly lifted, aimed his crossbow at the bailiff's back.

"Halt!" ordered the hunter, quiet but firm. "If one sole

step dost thou venture, the point of my arrow shall be the
last thou knowest of this dark world. Now, be still and tell
me soft who thou art!"

And like an arrow but truer of aim did the question hit
its mark, opening a wound of doubt in the mind of the bailiff, who knew not how to answer. For aside from the danger of his interrogant hailing from Úbeda, as he feared was
the case, what could he say? Ought he answer: I am the
thief from whom you have robbed what is yours? And if the
man was not from Úbeda, what then? I am Juan de Medina
Zevallos or Ceballos or Zavallos, depending on the source
consulted, and even, in certain documents, Francisco de
Medina Zeballos?

"I know not," answered scarcely audible the bailiff,
knowing not to whom he answered.

What other answer was there? Ought he have said
"Bailiff of the Royal Court"? Indeed, he answered surer to
his title than to his uncertain name. Scarcely less anony-
mous than his mules forgotten in the night, the bailiff noise-
less gleaned that he was naught but a mere function: he was
he whose honor it was to be commissioned by don Luis de
Mercado to transport the venerable body of a Carmelite
friar dead and smelling of saintliness, and being quite
frankly naught more than that, in losing it had he lost himself. Because who was the bailiff, really, if indeed he really
was. Who was he, beside a faithful servant and God-fearing
Christian avid for miracles that might lift him above the
unbearable flatness common among so many men of his

day, and without qualities beside a certain arrogance common among those of any day who hold lowly public office.
Who was he, beside a simple mule driver putting on courtly
airs? No one?

"I know not," answered the bailiff, for what else could
answer a character so faintly sketched, a character even
leaner of traits than his two dimwitted aides.

"You know not? Do you question who you are? Then
you must a philosopher be!" taunted the hunter under his
breath. "Answer me this, at least, Doctor Wantwit: have you
by chance seen a stag wounded by my arrow through these
woods pass?"

"Since abandoning the road to Madrid in search of the
highwayman who robbed me of my trunk I swear I have
seen neither man nor beast, I have seen no one, not even
you . . . "

"Turn, then, and look upon me, so that in looking upon
you might I know if you lie."

And in turning did the bailiff look upon the face of
the hunter, and it was as if two mirrors were set to face one
another. And in that infinite abyss did the bailiff see his
face copied in the face of that man whose crossbow at him
pointed, and he took the other to be death looking upon
him with his own eyes, and both did look away in fright.

"Tell me who thou art," entreated the bailiff, as starved
for self as he was afeared.

But the hunter answered not, for a sudden stag did
from the darkness emerge, interrupting the bewitching

bewilderment of indistinguishability. A great stag in great haste. A beautiful stag. And after the stag did the hunter quick and quiet set out, but not without turning to look upon himself once more. And the bailiff saw himself glossed as a hunter lost in pursuit of the stag, and the hunter saw the stag lost in the darkness and in the darkness could no one be seen.

No one was there when Ferrán passed by.

But where no one appeared did Ferrán hear sounds that appeared to be moans. But moans were they not: they were laughter. But laughter were they not: they were whimpers. But whimpers were they not: they were tears. In the darkness sobbed a child in terror. It was Diego. He was bleeding from one arm. The wound was slight, vouched Ferrán in the pale starlight as the veil of clouds briefly lifted. The arrow of no one had glanced him, but it had not held in his flesh.

XVIII. On how metaphors collapse, or, wherein still lost in the darkness of the "Night" do Ferrán and Diego search for meaning or path and in tempting to look ahead where no ahead can be found, for those verses are nearing their end, though a poem never truly ends but instead returns to its first silence and in that hushed darkness finds its beginning anew, the pair fails to note the impressive stones that hang suspended above their heads in a mercy that will not last.

"Shut up, will you?"

"Ferrán, I swear I wasn't crying."

"Shut your mouth, I say!"

"But I wasn't crying: I was praying with great fervor to the Virgin Mary that we might be granted the mercy of finding the friar's body."

"I know what I saw, and I know you to be not only a slut and a poof but also a cowardly capon incapable of suffering even the slightest scratch with honor. But fear not, safe will I keep your secret if you promise to shut your mouth for what remains of the night."

"So you promise not to tell the bailiff you found me crying?"

"Do you want me to tell him?"

"No! No, I beg you!"

"Shut up, then, and free my ears from the odious distraction of your voice, that they might serve as eyes in this darkness."

Through the darkness wandered Ferrán and Diego. Searching for the body of the friar they wandered. Or searching for the bailiff. Or searching for they no longer knew what. And despite feeling that they moved farther from their terror as they wandered, and though true it was that the company somewhat lightened the dark events that had each befallen, events so dark and so secret that neither dared not speak them aloud, each step in fact brought them deeper into the blackness where one step could not the next divine, and so like blind men lurching their way forward did they wander.

"I'm no poof, Ferrán."

"Poof, poofter, puff, ponce, fairy, buggerer, softling, sodomite—pick the one that suits your talents but kindly do shut up!"

"The blind man, though, he was. A poof, that is. Heard you not how he clamored for his beloved? And how his beloved was a man?"

"I would vouch that the beloved for whom the blind man, so shrewd and so false, claimed to be searching was none other than the friar himself, and that at this very moment is he reveling in his booty on the road back to Úbeda."

"Are you saying that the friar and the blind man . . . ?"

"What I am saying is that we should have let that shepherdess eat your tongue so I might now be spared the foolery of your words," said Ferrán, and while he spoke he stumbled and would indeed have fallen were Diego not at his side.

"You see? Look at what you do!" Ferrán chided Diego while to Diego he clung.

"No. I see not what I do because I see naught. I am blind! Blind!"

"You are not blind. Quit your foolery."

"How do you know?"

"Because you are not blind: it is just the night in our eyes."

"I wish I were blind!"

"Shut your mouth."

"I wish I were blind so I need not see this terrible darkness. This must be the Godless night of which the Devil warned us!"

"There you go, crying again."

"I'm no poof and I'll swear it, but that I am not a blind wretch I cannot vouch."

"Quit your sniveling."

"Do you see anything?"

"Do shut up."

"Doesn't it seem we've stumbled here before?"

"Shut up I say!"

"What if instead of stumbling further we paused for a moment to light a fire?"

"With what kindling? The twigs you tote in your nock-hole, poof?"

"Perhaps not a fire, then, but we could at least stir the spark that lies dormant in our flint, that it might briefly illuminate the truth of whether I am truly or falsely blind, whether what I see is the darkness of the night, or see not the darkness but wander blind through the night . . . "

"And how will you know that, dunce?"

"How's that?"

"How, in this unbroken darkness, will you know the difference between an absent sense of sight and a tempted but failed spark?"

"I don't understand . . . "

"If blind you truly are, how will you distinguish a spark from its absence?"

"All is lost!"

"Quit your shouting! Quiet, lest the townsfolk of Úbeda hear us all the way in Úbeda."

"We will be forever lost in the pitch-dark night!"

"Shut up, Diego, for the love of God, shut up!"

"We will be forever lost and like that blind man will I wander through the blackness begging for the eyes of my beloved!"

"You poof! I knew it! You shameless, impenitent poof!"

"Wait! Lo, I think I see something!"

"What do you mean?"

"I can see! Look!"

"Where?"

"There! Do you see it?"

"No. What? Where?"

"There! There!"

"Where's there?"

"There! There ahead!"

"I see nothing."

"Are you blind?"

"What do you see?"

"I know not . . . Shadows, but lighter. Figures I can't quite make out . . . Wait! 'Tis people!"

"What?"

"Yes, look! People! Travelers lost like us in the dark!"

"I see no one."

"Ferrán! Ferrán! Look! It's the bailiff!"

"Are you certain?"

"Hey! Hey! Over here! Don Juan, we're over here!"

"I see him not."

"Sweet mother!"

"What is it?"

"My God, oh my God!"

"Diego, talk to me! What the hell is wrong with you?"

But heavy blows to their pates cut short these words and obliged the pair to leave this pleasant exchange for a more favorable moment, as suddenly did they find themselves occupied with crumpling, fainting, and dropping face-first to the ground.

XIX. Wherein verses of the "Canticle" spring from Diego's mouth, though one might say these were by the friar's tongue recited, as if the friar had concealed himself in the body of the lad just as happens when the lover in the poem searches for her beloved outside and finds him not, because her beloved has hidden himself inside her, but then she arrives at a crystalline fount with this otherness within and sees herself or himself or themselves reflected in its waters, and secretly sung by his or her or their lips does this otherness peer out and is manifested and reflected and reads: "may your silvery surface / reveal now the sight / of those eyes most desired / which are sketched upon my heart!"

"Where have ye the saint's body hidden?"

There they were, gathered once more, the three members of a formerly secret order: the Society of the Stag, the Brotherhood of the Pitch-Dark Night, the Worshippers of the Wounded Heart, the Disciples of the Flesh, the Acolytes of the Dove, the Pilgrims of the Mysterious Verse, the Guardians of the Celestial Scent, the Sect of Sacred Nothings, the Knights of the Cadaver, the Thieves of the Missing Body. There they were, naked and bleeding and, to judge by their wounds, perhaps with a few broken bones:

the bailiff, Ferrán, and Diego, tied to trees like the painted icons of martyrs.

Their fears had at last come true: the townsfolk of Úbeda had overtaken them and had taken them captive. There they all were, the butchers with their knives, the pimps with their daggers, the jewelers with their chisels and with their tongs the blacksmiths, the carpenters with their saws and with their clippers the seamstresses, all inclined to interrogate the three with their blades.

"Where have ye the saint's body hidden?" asked again a man who had until that moment been a mercer but found more to his taste the role of Grand Inquisitor.

From sunrise had they been interrogated and debased, interrogated and whipped, interrogated and wounded with growing ferocity as they tempted time and again to explain, with words reddened by blood, that for which they had no explanation.

"As we told you, the friar's body is from our sight likewise hidden, for a blind man crossed our path in the night and thereafter did it vanish in a manner most supernatural," the bailiff vouched once more, no longer seeking to convince.

"Speak truthful," insisted the Inquisitor. "Where have ye hidden the body of Fray Juan de la Cruz?"

"As we told you, if you have it not we know not who might, and rather would I that you had it, for at least then would I know where and with whom it was, and closer at hand would it be," replied the bailiff with a sincerity born of despair.

At the Inquisitor's signal, a hardy merchant struck the bailiff's face with a cudgel.

"Tell us where ye have hidden it, lest we trade three corpses for one," insisted the Inquisitor.

But, driveling saliva and blood, the bailiff could muster no answer but the tooth that from his mouth sprung.

Between his stupefaction from the blows and exhaustion and terror and agony, the bailiff thought, disjointed and spasmodically, about don Luis and his lost honor, and how he would rather they just finish him off, but also about the daughter he would never see again; Ferrán thought about the knife taken from him and his sword so far from reach, about ropes pulled tight, about distant autos-da-fé, about his preparations to set out for the Indies, and about the Indies, increasingly remote; Diego thought about his parents and about sweet fritters, so as not to think about the events that had unfolded the night before or those presently unfolding, and about morcillas and sardines, but then again, maybe not morcillas and sardines for he was so very thirsty, more thirsty than he was hungry, really, so he thought about a crystalline fount, and about poor wounded Ferrán, and about a stag.

"Pesterers, phonies, vile lie-mongers, all! Speak true for once!" shrieked a Fury disguised as a sanctimonious old lady.

"Despicable, devil-sent pilferers! Give us back our friar!" cawed another dressed in mourning.

"Saintstealers! Cloisterthieves! Lutherans!" hissed another, more furious and darker still.

And spurred on by the shrieks of the old women, and eager in their own right, and finding no better license for cruelty than a just endeavor, particularly one celebrated by many, and taking theirs to be such and having no reason to think otherwise, several townsfolk of Úbeda readied their irons in the fire for an inquiry by cautery. Meanwhile the hardy merchant, who had been debating between a lock-pick and a dagger—seasoned pupil of malice that he was, deftly did he alternate suspense and surprise—raised an unexpected set of pliers for Ferrán to see.

"Where have ye the saint's body hidden?" repeated the Inquisitor.

"You waste a day of rage on us when you could be overtaking the blind man who robbed us and is now many leagues away," replied Ferrán, trembling at the sight of the instrument.

"A blind man, you say! A blind man! What sort of blind man could best the three of you and escape victorious into the pitch-dark night with the saint on his back?" interjected a cook brandishing a spoon.

"A false one," maintained Ferrán.

"False thy account, and if you tell us not where the body is hid will I with this spoon gouge out your peepers and remedy your cockeyed deceits with the truth of a very real blindling," threatened the cook, delighting in her recipe as if, having stewed and garnished those eyes most desired, her revenge was cooling on the plate.

"Save thyself toil, agonies, and afflictions, my child, and

tell us wherein it is hidden," asked calm the erstwhile mercer, his Inquisitor's air ever more honed.

"I cannot tell you what I do not . . . " Ferrán began to say but could not finish because the merchant with his pliers had wrenched his nipple, wringing from him an animal howl and leaving him in moans that were a great sorrow to hear.

"In the figure of a fleeing stag!" Diego interjected, that Ferrán might flee the question astride the stag in his answer.

"Where, do you say?" asked the bewildered Inquisitor.

"In the whisper of a loving breeze" said Diego, knowing not what he said.

"Where?"

"In the lone lock of hair you glimpsed stirring on my neck."

The executioner was poised to satisfy his pliers with Diego's flesh when the Inquisitor stayed his hand, sensing some truth of the friar in that gibberish.

"Wherein dost thou say the blessed corpse of Fray Juan is hidden?"

"In caverns of stone up high. In beauteous groves. In lonely wooded vales."

"What groves, what vales, what caverns? Speak clear! Where have ye hidden him?"

"In flowers and rose bushes, in the pleasant garden long desired, in the wine cellar, on a quiet night, upon your silvery surface."

"Quit this foolery and tell me clear: where is the body of the saint?"

"On the mount, in babbling brooks, on my budding breast."

He was delirious. Delirious with fear, with fever, with hunger, exhaustion, and love. But through his deliria did Diego speak truth as if by the tongue of another. For his deliria were none other than Fray Juan's liras and, though Diego knew them not, from him did they spring forth as if from an old and distant void or night or heart.

"Impudent scamp! If you tell us not forthwith where ye hid the body I shall bid sundered thy tongue and thou shalt with yon blades be probed until thy insides speak for thee through the mouth of your wound!"

"By this gracious lyre," raved Diego. "In the one that starts with the fields and ends with your saying I am lost. In the rhyme between dove and love . . . "

And so, unbeknownst to himself and in somewhat mutilated and glossed and spurious form, did Diego answer the query with figures and lines from the "Canticle," and better answer could there be none, for where else might the body of Fray Juan de la Cruz be found if not within his verse.

But the townsfolk of Úbeda were in no mood for commentaries. And hearing the body they saw it not and smelled it not, and hearing the body they knew it not, nor did they delight in its flesh, though the secret those lines carried of the friar did greatly their yearnings kindle.

Before feeling the pain, Diego, delirious with liras and stammering verses, received notice of the cautery from a scent of scorched hair and flesh he was slow to know as his own. A frantic tanner had quelled his fever by cooling his hot iron on the lad's breast in hope of speeding the friar's body to his tongue, not noticing how upon that tongue wounded by a kiss from Philomela was the friar's body already singing.

> *And the lone turtledove*
> *at last did find its love*
> *upon the verdant shore.*

XX. Wherein, following the commentary on the verses of the "Canticle," that which befell the body of the friar is explained, although—being as there are a great many versions and several among these being quite contradictory, such as one which anonymously attests that it was the bailiff himself who hid the body to protect it from the townsfolk of Úbeda, or the account offered by Fray José de Velasco in his biography of the friar, which contends that the townsfolk of Úbeda "sent men after the bailiff and, upon finding him at a lodging house while searching for the sacred body, our Lord vanished right before their eyes such that they could find him not, and so they took their leave," which coincides in substance with what has here been recounted, though not without modification, wonders being here trimmed or there bolstered—there is no more faithful account of the inexplicable than the multitude of these variations, which nonetheless serve as a commentary on and testament to the impossible, uncertainty being the effect of their overabundant truth.

A little boy staring at him agape: this was the first thing Ferrán saw as he coaxed his eyes half open. Ow, his eyelids. Ow, every organ and gland. Every vein hurt, every bone; his balls, fortunately still in place, hurt. Every muscle and every hair: ow. The only part that pained him not were his hands, so tightly tethered they had long ago gone numb. The whole of him, tethered to a tree. With the sun shining and the birds in song.

"The priest says he awaits you in church and that you should make haste," said the boy very slowly and very obediently and very focused on each word lest he err in transmitting the message.

A child? A priest? A church? And what of the townsfolk of Úbeda? Ferrán looked around him but saw not his captors. He looked at the bailiff and Diego, who, though also entirely beaten and tethered, wandered untethered from the world through untamed dreams.

"Wait, lad! Wait!" Ferrán managed to beg of the boy who was already taking his leave. "Untie me."

The boy paused, turned, and laughed.

"Come on! Hurry up and untie me. What keeps you, ninny?"

The boy shook his head, quaking with laughter. What an urge to stomp him! Or to give him a little kick, at least.

"Untie me, lad!" Ferrán shouted, despite the dryness of his mouth. "Are you deaf? Untie me!"

What an urge to clip a supple green switch and whip that snicker right out of him!

"Untie me! For the love of God, lad, untie me! Name your price. A silver real? I must have some coins in my pack. Have you seen my pack? Did you see where they left my clothes? Do you know where we might find our mounts? I promise to give you a shiny new coin if you untie me . . .

Where are those ruffians who held us captive? Speak, lad! Answer me! Say something!"

"The priest says he awaits you in church and you should make haste," replied the boy, as if those were the only words he knew.

"All right, dummy: do you propose we go to the priest still tied to these trees? If you untether us not, we will remain captive here and your dear priest will take it that you did not deliver the message as instructed but instead deceived him, and what a mess that will be."

After giving much thought to this argument, and not without hesitations or struggle, the boy finally untied Ferrán, who had an awful time stirring at first. Ow: everything hurt. But how sweet it was to be from those rigors released, and there was little time for complaining, lest the townsfolk of Úbeda return. And so with all haste—ow, ow, ow—did Ferrán set to freeing his companions.

Diego was dreaming of a golden dove with silver wings that flew gleaming through the night like a shooting star, a feathered star that came to rest on the back of a stag that fled no longer, when he was awoken by Ferrán.

On his knees in the grass, freed in body from his tethers but captive still of despair, the bailiff seemed neither startled by the townsfolk of Úbeda's disappearance nor fearful of their return.

Had he dreamt the hunter who, with arrows aimed from a nearby hilltop, did their captors dispel? Or had it been the shepherds, armed with slings and stones, who came to their rescue? Among the biographers there is no consensus, but reason discreetly suggests attributing the retreat of the townsfolk of Úbeda to the fact that in discovering the truth they also discovered their undeniable failure: the three wretches they held prisoner were naught but thieved thieves who knew not where the friar was hidden and could offer naught but the gibberish coaxed from their agony. And thus, without the body of Fray Juan yet partly revenged, with their pliers and their needles and their daggers and their irons and their fearsome clippers smeared with justice, had the townspeople of Úbeda taken their leave after exhausting their holy rage.

But the failure of those was not the victory of these: kneeling in the grass, head bowed and gaze blank, hands pressed to his temples as if supporting a terrible weight, the bailiff could have posed for a monument to defeat. His greatest fear had in the dark hours of their search turned to hope and then, in his captivity, was that hope turned to even greater despair: if the townsfolk of Úbeda held not the friar's body, he knew not who might, nor where he might begin to search. A sad thing it was to see so strong a man so vanquished.

"This pestilent runt claims a priest awaits us in church," said Ferrán, lacking words of solace for the bailiff.

"And that you must make haste," said the pestilent runt.

The two obeyed as if still captives, crossing the countryside behind Ferrán and the boy, though all three struggled greatly due to their many afflictions and wounds and injuries. Diego stumbled as if he were wandering blind through the dark night. The bailiff had the pitiable gait of a man about to be executed.

"And why does the priest want to see us?" asked Ferrán, between one ow and the next.

The boy laughed, shrugged, and continued on. Soon they reached a village freshly sprung from a bewitchment, or at least one they had not seen the night before when in the dark they passed by. It seemed like a place abandoned. At the edge of its deserted town square stood the church.

"Ah, but I nearly forgot the coin I promised you . . . Here it is!" said Ferrán, giving himself the gift of tipping the boy the hardest smack he could muster. "Would you like another?"

The boy ran off sobbing and was lost from sight.

"What kept you numbskulls? Have you not caused trouble enough? You must be quite proud of yourselves," the old priest, foul of mood, scolded from where he stood waiting in the doorway. "Good heavens! You might at least have covered your indignities first! But, nothing to be done . . . "

And allowing them neither to answer nor ask, nor affording them a moment's pause, he ushered them inside.

"Come, now! Make haste! Take what is yours and get out."

Heeding no earthly worriment and forgotten unto itself like a lily plucked, a hand pale as a lily and plucked of several petals or fingers peeked out from a trunk set like an offering at the altar.

"I know not how this arrived here nor who brought it. Ask me nothing, for I know nothing and wish to keep it thus. But no sooner had I stumbled upon this perfumed nuisance did I know it must have something to do with the fuss you raised out there in the woods. I know not what business you have here and I seek no trouble from supernatural authorities or earthly powers. So tell me nothing, for about nothing do I inquire. Take him swiftly hence, for the faithful will soon arrive and I must give mass. Hurry! Gather your cross and go! What keeps you?"

But the three men would no more petrified have been were it upon Medusa's head and not a saint's body they had set eyes.

Had the scene been carved into the church entryway to commemorate this wondrous discovery, the wall to the right of the door would bear the crests of the Mercado and Peñalosa families. Just above these, emerging from a forest of stone complete with a lavish profusion of monsters and angels and leafy motifs, would be visible three beautifully sculpted and greatly venerated nude men, the Brotherhood of the Pitch-Dark Night, guided by a clever youth who would point to the temple's door with one hand while holding in the other a tablet reading: "Give yourself to me at last / and think not to send / one herald more." On the other side would be seen the figure of a venerable old priest kneeling before a trunk crowned by rays of light with his arms spread in veneration and his gaze turned toward the lavishly wrought Virgin of Carmel, who would preside in all her glory over the scene. And in the center, above the arched doorway inscribed with the lines "You might say I am lost, / that wandering love-struck / I lost my way and was won," supported by a pair of well-crafted columns, a triangular pediment bearing at its apex the coat of arms of the Carmelite Order with its three stars would bridge one scene and the other, a pediment adorned with medallions at either end of its base, one bearing the likeness of the prophet Elijah and the other that of Saint Teresa of Ávila, the triangle itself being a likeness of Mount Carmel, and there at its heart or center, precisely where the body of Fray Juan de la Cruz would be expected, would be naught but an empty niche: a hieroglyph of the Mystery of the Disappearance.

XXI. Wherein, apropos of a fountain in which the bailiff, Diego, and Ferrán quench their thirst and cleanse their wounds, return is made to the first four lines of the twelfth verse of the "Canticle," which read, "O crystalline fount, / may your silvery surface / reveal now the sight / of those eyes most desired" and a commentary is offered thereon, whilst in the olden waters from which the poem drinks, descending into the deep above, Narcissus encounters Narcissus.

Two lions and two unicorns, no longer stone but rather the ghost of stone, driveled waters that had for centuries patiently worn them away. Waters in which Diego delighted, fresh as a bird. His bare, placid breast bore close to his heart the red mark of cautery. One might have likened him to a robin. The arrow's scrape was now a scar on his arm and upon his tongue Philomela's kiss was but a fading memory of pain.

Much relieved were they of their afflictions, as if the body of the friar had bestowed its grace upon them, or at least the bailiff liked to think it so; free, bold, and waiting for nightfall, the bailiff, Ferrán, and Diego paused their journey by that old fountain at the edge of the village to drink and replenish their stores and cleanse their wounds, and so the mules, recovered along with the rest of their luggage, might have a chance to cool off.

"Blind did I wander lost through the darkness!" cried the bailiff again and again, repenting his doubts and his flimsy faith. "Blind through the darkness did I wander, but now I see, so clearly do I see: by hiding the trunk from us, heaven freed us from the townspeople of Úbeda more surely than ever we could have done with our swords, and then returned it to us in improved condition, having been lightened of the foes it bore. Praise be to God our Lord!"

"A fickle goddess, truly, is Fortune, for in tempting to do us harm, the false blind man did us a great favor," said Ferrán, hoping to provoke with his needling some shift in the bailiff's psalm, the repetition of which had him especially vexed.

"Rightly do you call the blind man false," said the bailiff, taking the bait, "for now do I clearly see that he was no less than an angel draped in mortal rags and that blind were we who in our seeing saw naught. Believing that we saw, blind through the darkness did we wander!"

And, thinking the matter settled, the bailiff took his leave to indulge in solitude and silence. He would not allow the misgivings he had observed in his aide since early in their journey to detract from his celebration of this wonder. Surely Ferrán was already crafting an argument of discredence: that great must have been the false blind man's surprise upon opening the trunk to find a corpse instead of the lavish bounty he so desired, and that, blind to the treasure contained therein, he abandoned it in the church. Or something to that effect.

"Do you believe that blind man was really an angel in disguise?" Diego asked his companion.

"No."

"No?"

"No."

"But do you remember what he said?"

"What?"

"About how when he looked into the waters of the fount he saw the face of the fable of the other sketched upon it."

"No."

"You remember it not?"

"He said it not."

"What?"

"That was not what he said."

"What did he say, then?"

"Gibberish unworthy of our remembrance is what he said," said Ferrán.

And with that Ferrán turned and set to pissing beneath the indifferent sky. A living fountain at the fountain's edge. A moment's relief. A tepid stream. A joyful foaming quick to burst and evanesce.

"It is just that . . . Well, something like that happened to me as we wandered lost in search of the friar," said Diego, darkening asudden.

"What?" asked Ferrán, shaking off.

"What the blind man said about looking into the fable

of the fount and seeing sketched upon its waters the face of the other."

"That's not what you said."

"But it was the blind man who said it, not I."

"What I'm saying is that what you say the blind man said is not what you said the blind man said before."

"And what did I say?"

"That when he looked into the fount of the fable he saw the face of the waters sketched on the other."

"He said that?"

"You said that. Or that when the fable looked into the fount it saw sketched on its waters the face of the other, or that when the fable looked into the waters it saw sketched there the face of the fount, or that when it looked into the fount it saw sketched on its waters the fable's other face, or that when he saw himself sketched upon the waters of the fable the other looked into his own face, or that when the face of the other looked into the fount it saw the fable sketched upon its waters, or some such nonsense. I don't give a rat's farthing!"

"Well, you should, because it happened to us."

"It happened to us? What happened to us?"

"What the blind man said about how when he looked into the other he saw the face of the fable of the fount sketched upon his waters, or that when he saw himself sketched upon the waters of the fable the other looked out from the fount with his face or . . . I don't know! You con-fused me!"

"Ah, did I?" asked Ferrán, triumphant.

"All is since that night so confused! Beings and things seem to have shifted their very natures and, breaking free of their molds, matter and substance wander in unstable forms. No sooner do I tempt to say one thing but it is already another, and the words I speak do shift in my mouth and change while remaining the same. Does this not happen to you?"

"No."

"No?"

"No."

"And you suspect not, even in secret, that although we found the friar's body we might not have found it, or that you found me not in the night, or that you are not you nor I myself, though you and I are us and the body of the friar rests there in that trunk, as if we all wandered as copies in a mirror?"

"No."

"I mean, nor do I . . . What I meant to say was something else . . . You see? What I tempt in vain to say is this: On the night we searched for the friar as I wandered through the woods I stumbled upon a fount and near to it I drew to drink, for fear had dried my mouth, but when I looked into the dark mirror of its still waters, I saw what the blind man said."

"What?"

"That the fount looked into the other and saw sketched upon its face the fable of the waters, or . . . I know not, anymore. What I had meant to say was something else. What I had meant to say was that I saw your face sketched upon mine upon the face of the waters."

"My face? You must think me daft. Your face on my face? That's a rich one."

"'Tis true! I swear it! I were you or you was me or I know not what, but I saw myself in your face and your face saw me seeing itself. It was awful!"

"Awful? Awful? Then like the bailiff said, you must be the blind one, and not that wretched fake! Proof enough is this you've never once looked in a mirror. Awful? With that slack jaw, you wish my face were yours!" fumed Ferrán.

But no sooner had a misunderstood and rejected Diego lay down to nap in the sun, once the waters had stilled and he was certain that no one could see, did Ferrán pick up a stone. And untrusting did he approach the fount to confirm that his reflection his reflection remained. But when he approached the fount, he saw sketched upon its waters the face of the fable. But when the fount approached the fable of its waters, it saw the other sketched upon its face. But by approaching the other, the face of the fount of the fable was sketched upon the waters. And, casting its stone at the sky of the fount, the image shattered its mirror.

XXII. Wherein, as they walk the road to Madrid much relieved of their pursuers, Ferrán reveals to his companions his desire to set sail for the Indies as soon as their endeavor is completed and their recompense received, upon which Diego suggests that they go jointly, for he too is eager for such a journey, to which Ferrán responds with a perhaps and a let us discuss it anon and a silence falls between the two and they continue on their way, externally hushed but internally raucous with thoughts, emotions, dreams, and ambitions that keep them from partaking in the vast silence of the night wherein is expounded the fifteenth verse of the "Canticle," the third line of which secretly sighs a "gentle music."

Tranquil were the days that followed their recovery of the friar's body. Like a gift from Fray Juan himself after the many trials they had suffered due to his absence, crowed the bailiff. And thus lightly did they pass through Ciudad Real and Toledo. Those days knew no fear but that the heat and the sun's rays might rot the friar's flesh—whereupon the three maintained their precaution of moving only at night—and no misadventures but the meddlesome questions of travelers and busybodies. "What is it you port that hath so fine an odor?" they were asked on roads and in lodging houses. To which the bailiff, Ferrán, and Diego had learned to respond with requisite discretion without rousing the suspicions of those who upon them did thusly impose.

The restfulness of those days was aided by the flatness of the road through Castile, where at dusk the sun rolled across the sky like an orange across a country table, nudging them to continue on their way. But to say this is to say too much, for the flatness of Castile allowed neither ornamentation nor rhetorical flourishes, much less the luxury of metaphorical Andalusian oranges. Those days were, at most, brimming with the austere joys through which sages of all epochs have exercised the virtue of simplicity and the simple of spirit have found their greatest ease. And with the pleasant whisper of a breeze in the peaceful night and the sonorous solitude of the countryside.

But what serves the journey does not necessarily serve its narration, for though each journey is a lesson in letting go, and though a restful night free of remarkable events might well prove beneficial for the spirit, the reader will by the third description of such a night be yawning, and if not by the fourth then certainly by the fifth will have abandoned the book with many pages and verses and much road still ahead.

And given that continued flatness does also fatigue, and that in their crossing do the plains reveal themselves treacherous in their horizontal way, even the bailiff, Ferrán, and Diego began to tire of this serenity bland with lack of adventure, and to long for the seasoning of the supernatural.

This much can be gleaned, at least, from what the bailiff himself recounted years later to Fray Alonso de la Madre de Dios, as the friar states in his *Life, Virtues, and Miracles of the Holy Father Fray Juan de la Cruz*: "One night on their journey, as the weather was fair, Juan de Medina told his companions to leave the road so they and their mules might rest a while. And there, distanced from the road by a lush crop of wheat, they took of the grains they found and cast handfuls to their mounts, saying, 'Should the owner of these lands appear, we shall pay him fair.' After taking their rest awhile, they sensed people approaching with whispers through the wheat and the brush but could see no one. As they regarded these murmurs did a dog of purest white and great stature appear, tail wagging through the wheat, and it did move among them and their mounts as if it were of their company, drawing near to them and showing them affection as if they were known to it. And having done this several times, it took leave of them through the brush and was not seen again. Medina, cautious for his freight, said to his companions, 'I believe this dog has revealed itself by its comportment to be a thing of the Saint we bear, and that it has commanded we leave this place. And so let us make haste, for I fear our stay in these parts might bring a scuffle upon us.' And so they followed the path of the dog's retreat and, thusly guided, they returned to the road, which they followed without event all the way to Madrid."

Delightful, the visitation of this dog. Amusing, the visitation of this dog as recounted by the bailiff, though insufficient for securing the beatification of Fray Juan de la Cruz, as was the intention of Fray Alonso in gathering these statements. And yet a timely, providential visitation it was, relieving the dryness of the account with its wet nose, its pink tongue, and its curiosity, with the happy wag of its tail. Who could begrudge the bailiff his zealous attempt to take the hound for a messenger of supernatural powers, for who among us has not felt blessed when visited by the spontaneous affections of a dog? But the divide that separates the natural from the supernatural is far greater than the distance between Úbeda and Segovia, and if the dog had indeed a messenger been, its message was naught but the dog itself. And so just as he fed his mules with whatever was at hand, though his it was not, upon finding himself needful of wonders did the bailiff procure one from what was at hand, which was the dog. And, stroking the dog's coat, did he desire to take the grace of the ordinary for something extraordinary, though extraordinary was it not, and thus entangled in this artifice did he find in the extraordinary a justification for departing without paying for the grain he took.

This is no place to debate whether the Creator speaks to us in His glory through even the meekest of His creatures, as Fray Juan was wont to believe, or whether these creatures serve Him as mirrors. Likewise beyond these scribblings lies the question of whether a dog, as naught but a dog, a miracle in and of itself might be. Perhaps all is miracle or perhaps there are no miracles but those invented by need. Perhaps that which seems supernatural is naught but poetry. Who knows? But given that the poems of Fray Juan are of dogs entirely devoid, to take one as sign of the friar is at least a flight of fancy, if not a willful departure. In the bestiary of the friar's verse can be found horses, lions, stags, leaping does, foxes, turtledoves, hens, birds of prey, and lone fowl of unspecified color. But his poems are as lean of dogs as is lean of poetry the prose describing these flat days during which mere mortals filch, frazzle, and rest; days during which, distant the feats of saints and heroes, these men can seize no more than a handful of grain first borrowed then stolen. Peaceful days. Days without the jolt of extraordinary incidents. Days without rhyme, allegory, or simile. But days on which one might, at rest in a field of wheat, hear in the silence a gentle music or a zephyr hound fanning through the brush.

XXIII. *Wherein, by expounding the second line of the thirty-third verse of the "Canticle," which reads "if dark you found me of complexion" is the Jewish heritage of that line also pronounced, for its provenance is none but the Song of Songs, the translation of which from Hebrew into ottava rima by Fray Luis de León translated into inquisition and imprisonment for its translator, but which Fray Juan de la Cruz likely encountered along with the Vulgate during his studies in Salamanca, and which reads "I am dark of complexion but comely," though room there is to suspect that this darkness might contain a secret but suggested, a quelled and quarreled Moorish filiation, whereby the verse might not only be the cornerstone of synagogues but also be that of mosques, like the church tower stripped of Christian robes that bare declares its minaret beauty only to be later again draped in Christianity, and thus expounded does this line not so much comment upon as illuminate those that follow, which read, "now can you look on me well / for such beauty and grace did you leave in me / when your eyes upon me fell," though these words do not so much illuminate as whitewash and whiten the first line of a later verse, which reads "The little white dove," and in this whitening or lightening do they echo what would befall the body of Fray Juan de la Cruz, who, being in life dark*

138

of complexion or olive-skinned, grew lighter in death or did whiter appear, as was recounted at length much earlier in these commentaries.

Uncertain whether it was the will of don Luis that they should take lodging in Madrid or, to the contrary, carry on to Segovia without delay, and fretful of passing through so bustling a city in daylight, the bailiff chose to stop at a tavern or inn at its outskirts. To the home of the Royal Justice did he send Diego with a message, and in waiting for a response did the bailiff and Ferrán treat themselves to a nice wine.

How sweet the wine's fire coursing through their veins, how satisfying the knowledge that their task neared its end, how glad a tiding of future repose would have been their present repose had not a boisterous old countess and her servant—who though named Zoraida answered to wench, whore, villain, marrana, and all the other cruelties her mistress delighted in casting at her—sat themselves at their table.

"Has ever there been baser ruffians than these," the noblewoman wailed, "who in the presence of a countess offer not a drop of their wine in due deference to her station, age, and condition!"

"Please excuse our inelegance, Your Ladyship, if in the throes of our dealings insensitive we seemed to the privilege of your company," Ferrán rushed to say as he poured two more glasses, attentive to the bosoms of the comely servant.

And fawningly was Ferrán raising his glass to this shabby honor when the innkeeper did appear beside him, having found occasion to air his grievances.

"Careful with these two," he warned the men that the women might hear, "around them no caution is too great nor is the greatest fortune sufficient. Twenty days have they lodged here and nary a coin have I seen, though endless reverences and honors they do demand, and among the guests do they partake of all that is eaten and drunk whereby I hold that these two consume no less in a day than ten goatherds."

"Silence, you insatiable pig-bank," threatened the countess. "Close that slot you have for a mouth before my son's men arrive from Segovia to shove gold escudos down your miserable throat until you burst. As well you know, if my means are presently meager it is because the wanton hussy I have for a servant has robbed me blind. Thief! Thief! I demand justice! With these gentlemen as my witness, this odious Moor hath stolen my sapphire!"

"'Tis on your finger, Madam," replied Zoraida with the apathy of a comic performing her bit for the hundredth time. And with the apathy of a spectator who has seen that bit before did the innkeep make his way back to the kitchen.

"Not only a thief but stupid, too," said the countess, feigning surprise at the ring on her pinky. "Tell me, ninny, why steal my sapphire only to leave it where it was?"

"As the pawnbroker told you, Madam, that stone is but colored glass," retorted the servant.

"I should give the creature a good lashing, but alas I am old and too weak for it. Would you good gentlemen be so kind as to aid me with this arduous task?"

His good humor ruined, the bailiff would scarce lend the countess an ear much less an arm, but much did it unsettle Ferrán not to find the charge at all unappealing. Zoraida smiled lewd.

"Would it not be better to run her off, Your Ladyship?" asked Ferrán, desperate to escape the lash of desire.

"Unthinkable! How then would she repay all she owes me? For years now has she been chipping away at my fortune and my jewels. Of all my grand necklaces she has left me naught but this string of pearls as gapped as my poor old teeth. Oft have I reported her to the authorities, but just as she is a thief is she also a whore, and the harlot seduces the officers and judges who should be arresting her. So here I am, at her mercy, stranded at the outskirts of Madrid without a farthing, waiting to be rescued by my son's men."

"Ha! It is she who owes me a fortune," snapped Zoraida. "It must be years since last I saw any pay but blows with her shoe and pinching and roughness."

"Why, then, do you not leave her?" Ferrán asked, insinuating perchance an invitation.

"Christian charity. She has no one to care for her. She would not last an hour."

"Who are you to speak of Christian charity, you perfidious Moor!" the countess erupted. "A thief and a whore are you, and moreover a liar, a fake, and a scallywag! A daughter and granddaughter of Moors, if not of Jews. Marrana! Upon my honor, in all her years of service this false Christian has prepared my garbanzos, beans, and lentil stews like a Moor, leaving me in the state of famishment you good gentlemen see before you."

As if her religious barbs were at his person aimed, Ferrán felt himself in danger with his lineage nigh revealed, and the black pool which had on like occasions grown until it clouded his mind entire was threatening already to spread when his gaze fell upon Zoraida's ebony eyes. And deep in their blackness flashed a whip of light. And Ferrán felt himself bound to Zoraida by an incestuous kinship. How he longed to have ready his false certificate of blood purity with its genuine seal and to set out posthaste for the Indies, bringing the dark of complexion and much suspected Zoraida with him.

"Had Madam provided the monies for bacon, gladly would I have prepared your stews like a Christian," the servant explained.

"Christian stew, Jewish stew. Ha! Jew stew, how clever," cackled the countess, pouring herself more wine in celebration of her wit. "But mark: no sooner have I foot in Segovia will I turn you over to the Holy Inquisition. Let them decide whether you are Moor or Jew."

"I fear, Madam," said Zoraida, "that we are hard bound to our debts in this place, never to reach Segovia. And furthermore," she added, savoring the misfortune, "that your ungrateful son, ignoring your pleas and his filial duties, has sent no one as emissary of his aberrant indifference."

"Tell me, kind sirs, are you not on your way to Segovia? For I would vouch that I heard something to that effect moments ago," probed the countess with her back to her servant. "Or where is it you are taking those hams?"

"Hams? What hams?" stammered Ferrán.

"The legs of ham you carry in your trunk, which waft so fine a scent," the countess insisted, now quite sure of herself.

A discreet kick from Ferrán cried mute for aid and put the bailiff on guard, but skilled as he was at answering for flowers and perfumes he too lacked the art to explain away a ham. Hams! Good heavens. Hams? Who could mistake flesh as holy as that of Fray Juan de la Cruz for a ham? Though it must be said, the bailiff gravely reflected, some hams do of glory taste.

"I see that you gentlemen are agitated," jabbed victorious the countess. "Of what are you afeared? That I might report you, as well? Are these perchance stolen meats?"

"We know not of what hams Your Ladyship doth speak," ventured Ferrán, still awaiting the bailiff's intervention.

"Those are not hams, Madam, 'tis but your hunger manifesting thus in your nose," interjected Zoraida. "We have been two days without a bite to eat," she said, turning toward the men, "for that heartless innkeep refuses us even crusts and scraps. But my mistress is not blinded by hunger when for thieves she takes you, at least, not when it comes to thee," she added, suddenly fierce and addressing only Ferrán.

"What are you saying, woman?" cried Ferrán, incredulous, exposed, guilty, surprised, furious, betrayed, brokenhearted.

"Better were it for you that I spoke not," Zoraida challenged him, prideful.

"If you wish me not to speak, better were it for you to fill my mouth with ham," threatened the countess.

"Speak all ye will, we have no ham upon us," the bailiff managed to stammer.

"You fool me not! I know the smell of a good Iberian ham," salivated the countess, "and I will settle for no less than a leg."

"'Tis not ham but flowers, or rather deflowerings, that you smell. I could sniff this one out from leagues away as a thief of honor and a robber of love," said Zoraida, pointing at Ferrán. "A libertine who offers poems and songs and ribbons and a thousand little trinkets in exchange for a maiden's heart and hymen, only to scorn her thereafter. Rogue, do you think I marked not the intentions behind your gaze?"

"What know you of hymens, Shulamite?" cackled the countess. "What know you of honor, you wench, deflowered by the suitors of that whore your mother while you were still in the womb. Flowers? Honor? Hymens? My ass. By the Blessed Virgin, those are hams!"

Never before had Diego been to the bailiff so welcome a sight. The lad returned bearing word that they were to lodge in Madrid, at the convent of the Discalced Carmelites in the Plaza de Santa Ana, for don Luis and doña Ana did wish to bestow upon the sisters of the Order, for a time, the pleasure of the friar's body. And though he understood the friar's body to be the cause of this great ruckus, Diego could not for the life of him fathom why it was hams this and hams that; nor did he find the women agreeable, least of all the servant woman for how she looked at Ferrán and hurled insults his way. And so with all haste did they load the mules and set to the road, even as the women followed them shouting.

"Do the Crown and all of Christendom a service," yelled the countess, nearly out of breath, "and leave us at least one slice of ham that this marrana, in rejecting it, might reveal herself to all as the false Christian she is . . . "

"And you would just leave me like this, libertine?" Zoraida hurled a final curse at Ferrán, lifting her skirts well above her immodesty. "May thy tongue be forever sunk into darkness!"

XXIV. Wherein Diego, waiting with his companions for the doors of the convent of Santa Ana to be opened to them, entertains himself by scattering with stomps the doves which in that plaza abound, and the terrified flight of these birds offers a commentary on that of the Bride in the "Canticle," who, at the beginning of the thirteenth verse, having found those eyes she so desperately sought just a few lines earlier, rather than delighting in their finding exclaims in terror, "Look away, my Beloved, / for I take to wing!" though this exclamation is caught mid-air by the Bridegroom and answered in that same second line with, "Return, my dove," seizing with these words the flight of which she speaks, defying hemistich and caesura as he joins and commingles with and participates in those same airs, for what is the "Return" he utters if not the Bridegroom's own return to the flight of the Bride, who now in the air of his utterance is turned.

No sooner had the venerable Madre Ana de Jesús breathed in that delicate perfume did she know it was Fray Juan de la Cruz that wafted her way.

Fray Alonso de la Madre de Dios proffers details: "Before entering Madrid did Medina send word to don Luis de Mercado and his sister doña Ana, for nearby with the holy body he awaited either instructions regarding whence

146

to convey it or orders to proceed to Segovia without delay. Doña Ana responded that they should to the convent of the Discalced Carmelites deliver it, and that she would await them there. Then did she send word to Padre Fray Blas de San Alberto, Vicar and Definitor in the absence of Padre Nicolás de Jesús María, the latter having traveled to Italy for the general chapter being held in Cremona, entreating him to grace them with his presence among the Discalced, that there in the convent they might have dealings. The Vicar arrived at the convent with his companion and doña Ana at the same moment as the holy body. He instructed the portress to bring the Reverend Mother Ana de Jesús, who was prioress there, but revealed not to what end. As they lowered the holy body from the mount upon which it had arrived, it gave off a most delicate aroma and fragrance that filled the entryway and through the convent entire did spread. In her quarters did the venerable prioress smell this fragrance and, knowing neither what had occurred nor that the body most desired awaited in the entryway, commented to the nuns who accompanied her and who smelled that same perfume: 'That is the scent of Fray Juan de la Cruz.'"

However valuable his account, Fray Alonso errs in calling the most venerable Ana a prioress, either from excusable ignorance, those being days of tumult and confusion for the Discalced, or from honorific habit, as founder and prioress of that convent had she for several years been. Or perhaps it was not an error but rather a daring thrust of poetic justice, an attempt to correct in the pages of his

volume the errors of the world, for as a prioress her gifts
and merits were as many as were her followers among the
Discalced Carmelites. Outside Fray Alonso's writings, however, it had been two years since Madre Ana's demotion and
imprisonment in the convent for her rejection of the new
Constitutions proposed by the Vicar Fray Nicolás, as they
ran contrary to the thought of Teresa de Jesús, and for leading a revolt that had won her, along with her captivity, the
sobriquet "Captain."

Had it harmed their friendship that early in the revolt
Fray Juan turned a deaf ear to her grievances? Yet also is it
true that later did he valiantly defend her cause at the general chapter of the Order convened in 1591 in Madrid, and
that this defense brought the friar great misfortune and
powerful enemies and much did hasten his end. His initial
reluctance to pronounce himself might be credited to the
detachment for which he was known and to his great repug-
nance of any noise that might distract him from his prayers.
Perhaps it was these very qualities that, years earlier, had
disappointed Teresa de Jesús, though she always took the
friar to be most holy. Fray Juan was not a man of action.
Too spiritual for Teresa's taste, too contemplative, pas-
sive—effeminate, even, according to some—not to men-
tion slight, slim, gaunt, humorless, bland. In a word, Fray
Juan was no Padre Jerónimo Gracián—so tall, so striking,
so virile, so elegant—for whom Teresa had a terrible weak-
ness, which had given rise to all manner of murmurings.
"Never have I seen such perfection with such sweetness

united," she wrote upon meeting the blue-eyed charmer. Teresa addressed Gracián as Eliseo or Paul in letters she would sign, with no small dose of flirtation, as Angélica or Laurencia. Fray Juan, on the other hand, was "my little Seneca," as if her initial admiration were shrinking to a vanishing point somewhere between mockery and affection. But now Fray Juan was dead. But now Gracián wandered the century, expelled from the Order by Fray Nicolás. But now Teresa was no more than a wisp of froth in the sky, an airy sigh of marble, a hallucinated sculpture of haze pierced by a dart of light: the caprice of a cloud seen by no one but Ana de Jesús, who often watched it writhe in the heavens through the tiny window of her misfortune.

"That is the scent of Fray Juan!" the venerable Ana, briefly freed from her prison, exclaimed once more upon reaching the entryway. Past the lattice that separated her from the locutorium were gathered around the friar's body, as was earlier affirmed, don Luis and doña Ana, Fray Blas and his companion, and the bailiff, whom the venerable Ana de Jesús did not know. A bit farther back, by the gate, in whispers argued two laymen, Ferrán and Diego, whom likewise she knew not. "Those two lads are from the blind man sent; they will guide you through places unknown, hidden from the eyes of God," thought the venerable Ana in the words of Fray Juan no sooner had she seen them, and in her mind did she expound the phrase as if offering a commentary to Fray Juan. This happened on occasion while the friar still lived, and it was said that thusly did they continue their communication in secret.

The eyes of doña Ana de Mercado y Peñalosa met those of the most venerable Ana de Jesús. Both were the spiritual daughters of Fray Juan and Fray Juan had done each the honor of dedicating to her a book. Did the two secretly harbor the rivalry of sisters? Had doña Ana insisted on the body's hiatus among the Discalced to console the venerable Ana in her moment of suffering, or had she wished under guise of generosity to inflict further wounds by flaunting her final possession of the friar? "We women are not so easily understood," scribbled Teresa de Jesús on a slip of paper, mocking the arrogance of the prelates, "men spend years hearing our confessions and later are shocked by how little they grasped." But now Teresa was dead. But now Fray Juan was dead, as the eyes of the most venerable Ana did vouch. And Ana did lower her eyes that their gaze might not be gazed upon. Were those strange yearnings the welling of tears? Why, then, did these waters wound her as fire?

XXV. Wherein, under the auspices of the first line of the thirty-sixth verse of the "Canticle," which reads "Let us one another enjoy, my Beloved," do the nuns of Santa Ana enjoy not only the contemplation of the body of Fray Juan but also its cleansing, as diligent and zealous they hastily—though the moments afforded them for this mercy fly hastier still—free him of his lamentable tatters, scrub from his bareness the lye by which the brethren had turned it white, wash blood and dirt from flesh and locks and comb the latter, along with his beard, and the perfume emanating from his body is so good indeed that fevered with its scent do they find themselves needful of escape to the patio and breaths of fresh air and water from the fount sprinkled on their faces so that, composed once more, they might return to the body beloved and enjoy once more its cleansing, and so fully do they enjoy and so fully is the verse expounded that well might it have read, "Let us one another expound, my Beloved."

The Vicar and don Luis and doña Ana had departed. Departed too was the bailiff on a visit to his kin, having instructed Ferrán and Diego to transport the body to the home of doña Ana once the time allotted the nuns had passed, for it was the will of don Luis that it should there

spend the night. And Ferrán and Diego awaited this passing of time in the convent stables, sprawled on the hay with
no company but their mules. To liven the wait, Ferrán, free
of the bailiff's censure and true to his way, recited these airs
parodic with nunnish voice and manner:

> *With no soldier shall I go,*
> *much less with any rogue;*
> *I'd rather have Fray Juan by me*
> *than swoon to any ogre.*
> *Tho perhaps my dear betrothed*
> *doth not stately measure,*
> *a loving year with the friar engrossed*
> *will surely bring me pleasure.*

"What a great poet you are!" acclaimed Diego amid
laughter and applause.

"Hardly," replied Ferrán. "'Tis not my verse, dimwit. I
heard it here on the delectable lips of a hazel-eyed novice."

"A novice?"

"Why so surprised, ninny? Nuns are famous for their
talent at threading the needle. They like their asparagus as
much as the next lass."

"Asparagus?"

"Now, I needed to make a few improvements here and
there . . . "

"Improvements?"

"Trifles. An inflection here, a syllable there . . . "

"And did you also improve the friar's measure, or by chance did nature match meter?"

Ferrán looked curious upon Diego, as if trying to respond less to the lad's question than to the simple riddle of his person. Then, having thought on it a moment, he smiled and for an answer extracted a small bundle from the bottom of his saddlebag.

"See for yourself!" he said, tossing the mysterious parcel to Diego.

Diego caught the enigma mid-air but grasped its nature neither in its catching nor in its unwrapping, which revealed a dry piece of flesh.

"Well, how does it measure? Big, ordinary, small, saucy?" asked Ferrán, amused by his friend's agitation.

"I know not . . . I know not how you could dare, how you could presume . . . How could you?" stammered Diego, knowing and not knowing, offended, horrified.

"Though in such a state of relaxation futile would it be to seek a fair verdict, except, perhaps, for a courtesan of great expertise. Perhaps were you to kiss it with due faith and devotion might you witness the miracle of the resurrection of the flesh and behold it in its full glory . . . "

"Kiss it yourself, if such is your faith," parried Diego.

"You first, you cock-worshipping knave. Gladly would you hold one on your tongue each Sunday like Communion if such grace were bestowed upon you. Lo! Behold! The friar's tonsured head doth peek from its fleshy hood!"

Diego looked down with equal measure of horror and

hope to find naught but the same plump chunk of flesh, inert in his hand.

"What a ninny you are," mocked Ferrán. "A ninny and a false convert. But we shall not want for sisters less prim of nature to offer proof of their faith, sisters who would enjoy venerating the relic of this holy coxcomb. The great commotion stirred in the cloister by his body offers a propitious occasion to find the nun of whom I spoke, and the relic offers a means to draw her from the others. Once I have her in secret shall I my own cock display beside the friar's, that she might kneel and worship according to the measure of her devotion."

Ferrán's cock pointing like a knife at the kneeling nun, Ferrán's knife slicing the friar's cock, the friar's cock in Diego's sweaty palm, Diego kindled with strange yearnings—all this, in brief, was too much for Diego's feeble youth. And he felt himself cave in, crack up, give out, and oh what confusion, what commotion, what captivation as he felt his sensual parts move indecorous and grow and rise. It must be the friar's doing, thought Diego, tempting to find a supernatural cause for his errant tumescence. It must be, repeated he frantic as he gripped fast the chunk of Fray Juan de la Cruz, whose body and scent do spirit and mind bestir and dark loves do kindle.

But was the blessed body of Fray Juan truly of this stiffness the cause and motor? Were this verily so would Fray Juan himself call it "spiritual licentiousness," the secret communication between flesh and soul to which the friar kindly dedicates several pages of his commentary on the Night: *For often it comes to pass that, during one's spiritual exercises, through no act of one's own, there arise and occur in one's sensual parts indecorous movements, sometimes even when the spirit is deep in prayer or engaged in the Sacrament of Penitence, or in the Eucharist. These things are not, as I say, within one's power to control [. . .] They often proceed from the pleasure which man takes in spiritual things, for when the spirit and the sense are pleased, every part of a man is moved by that pleasure according to its proportion and nature. For in that moment the spirit, which is the higher part, is moved to pleasure and delight in God, while the sensual part, which is the lower of the two, is moved in pleasure and sensual delight, for as it can take hold of naught else it takes hold of what is nearest to it, which is indecorous sensuality [. . .] There are also souls so tender and feeble of nature that when any spiritual grace comes to them it is transformed within them into spiritual licentiousness, inebriating and delighting their sensual parts in such manner that they are as if plunged into the nectar and pleasure of this vice, and grace and delight remain intertwined, passively; on certain occasions, unruly and indecorous acts are said to have taken place. The cause is that these souls, being as I say tender and feeble, are bestirred in their humors and blood by the least provocation, and hence arise these movements* . . . One might argue, to Diego's great relief, that—given his tender and feeble nature, which has been amply evidenced—the lad's wayward tumescence was merely a recital of the friar's words by his own flesh.

"Ninny! Oh, but you are a ninny," said Ferrán, taking pity on his friend's pained expression. "'Tis not his dick."

"What?" said Diego, wresting himself from his stupor.

"'Tis not the friar's dick, ninny."

"Whose is it, then?" asked Diego, dropping the chunk of flesh from his grip as if it were suddenly scalding.

"The friar's."

"I don't understand. It is not the friar's dick but it is the friar's? What do you mean?"

"I mean you are a ninny. 'Tis not the friar's dick, but his tongue."

"His tongue?"

"His tongue, ninny. What kind of ass cannot tell a cock from a tongue?"

"Ah," sighed Diego in relief or disappointment. "His tongue."

"I wager it will bring a goodly sum, enough to cover all the injury and fatigue and labor unforeseen when we set our wage with the bailiff. Fair is fair. But the friar's dick I want for myself. The night shall not pass ere I with this knife do maraud his rod."

"His rod?"

"His rod and its cohort, and you're going to help me."

"Me?" squeaked Diego, so engorged that he feared he might climax without the aid of any hand.

"On this night, for we'll have no other, while don Luis and doña Ana slumber. We shall find no amulet more potent than the friar's dangles for stirring feminine favor.

Young and old, rich and poor, all have we seen kindled by his mere presence and perfume . . . Ninny, look not at me thus! Mark that he who fancies himself she would be well off without a rod, for truer spoken and in more wondrous delight would he spend the nights of his verse."

"His rod, his rod, his rod," repeated Diego as if tempting to root the word from his body.

"I'll have your rod if you breathe a word of this to the bailiff, for well do I know the measure of your tongue. And while I'm at it I'll sever that, too, so keep it tucked behind the fly of your lips."

XXVI. Wherein at the request of the most venerable Madre Ana de Jesús is readied a commentary on the second line of the thirty-sixth verse of the "Canticle," which reads "and we shall ourselves in your beauty behold," as an allegorical angel descends bearing a mirror in which no one is reflected.

Regarding the curious verse "and we shall ourselves in your beauty behold" Fray Juan de la Cruz offers the following commentary: *This means: let us proceed such that, through the exercise of love earlier described, we may behold ourselves in your beauty in eternal life, that is: in this way may I be in your beauty transformed, and, being alike in beauty, may we behold one another in your beauty that is become ours; and thus as each looks upon the other, might each behold their own beauty in the other, the beauty of one and of the other being your beauty alone, as absorbed am I by your beauty. And thus shall I see you in your beauty, and shall you see me in your beauty, and I shall see myself in you in your beauty, and you shall see yourself in me in your beauty; and thus might I resemble you in your beauty, and my beauty shall be your beauty and your beauty shall be mine; and thus shall I be you in your beauty and you shall be I in your beauty, for your beauty shall be my beauty and thus shall we behold ourselves in your beauty.*

"You don't understand it either, do you?"

Diego was returning from his search for the portress, from whom he sought word of the friar's body for the time agreed upon had passed, but now he found himself locating neither her nor the source of this question.

"No, you don't understand it. Is this not true, my child?"

The lad was at first uncertain whether these words were at him directed, but he took his ears for their aim given that there was no one else around and given, moreover, their general truth, for truly did he understand nothing, understanding as he was not even what or whom he was not understanding. Diego understood nothing, and even less after Ferrán's recent jokes, confidences, and threats, thus even more perplexed and obscured unto himself did he stumble blindly in search of that voice.

"Come here, my boy, that I might enliven my captivity in conversation with you."

Diego's eyes fell upon a shadow in the locutorium and obedient did he that darkness approach, seeking for his confusion a cure. From the far side of the lattice repeated the most venerable Ana de Jesús:

"Tell me, then. Does its meaning escape you, too?"

"Your Reverence! No, Your Reverence . . . I mean, yes, Your Reverence . . . Or I mean I know not, Your Reverence . . . Forgive my clumsiness, Your Reverence. What I meant is that if Your Reverence says so, then so must it be for truly I do not understand it," said Diego, bowing his head.

"Its meaning long escaped me, too; after many years and many words I still do not understand it, though I sense I am finally able to not understand it better. Is it not the same for you, my boy?"

"I could not say, Your Reverence, for I know not even what it is that I understand not."

"But, look! 'And we shall ourselves in your beauty behold.' Of what else are we speaking, my child, if not that obscure verse?"

"Forgive my ignorance, Your Reverence, but I know not the verse of which Your Reverence speaks, for as Your Reverence rightly says, it is most obscure. Forsooth I know no other verse by the holy Fray Juan but a poem they call the 'Night' and which I heard but once from the brethren of San Miguel longer ago, it seems, than the weeks marked by the calendar."

"Well, now is the line known to you. So, my child? Can you tell me what it means?"

Diego lowered his eyes, finding neither excuse nor apology nor precept in his meager repertory of gallantries.

"I deeply regret, Your Reverence, that I cannot grasp the meaning of . . . "

"No, no, my child. Regret it not, when not even Fray Juan could. I asked him myself, and do you know how he answered?"

"I know not, Your Reverence."

"Precisely! Those were his exact words! I know not, Your Reverence, was how Fray Juan replied when I asked him what secret tidings, what sweet explanations, what fond mysteries and truths were in his loving phrases and poems contained. And do you know what he said next?"

"What did he say, Your Reverence?"

"Nothing."

"Nothing?"

The most venerable Ana de Jesús paused with her eyes fixed on nothing and smiled, returning the smile of no one.

"Nothing!" she continued asudden. "Hundreds of pages expounding nothing, page upon page of that miraculous mind not knowing, of conveying without saying and of saying with silence. As if he had untethered his words that they might join together according to their own whim and accord, thereby allowing language to speak its obscure secret, which in the end is naught but nothing . . . Do you follow, my child?"

"I fear, Your Reverence, that I am lost."

"Are you versed in Scholastic theology, my child?"

"How could someone who cannot even write his name aspire to so high a science?"

"All the better! Nor am I. And do you know what Fray Juan wrote to me in the volume he composed upon my insistence? 'Though Your Reverence may be ignorant of Scholastic theology, by which divine truths are understood, ignorant are you not of mystic theology, which is learned through love, and by which these truths are not only known, but also relished.'"

Upon the Reverend Mother's lap lay a manuscript that

she stroked as if it were a wounded animal. A dove, perhaps. A dubious turtledove from which the lad could not wrest his eyes as he stared unblinking through the locutory lattice. This worn paper pet was, according to its cover, called *A Spiritual Canticle* and for an epigraph it bore the words *Commentary on the verses treating the exercise of love between the soul and Jesus Christ its Bridegroom, wherein are addressed and expounded certain points and effects of prayer; written at the request of the Reverend Mother Ana de Jesús, prioress of the Discalced Carmelite Convent of San José in Granada. Year of our Lord 1584.*

"My Sisters are off enjoying the body of Fray Juan, but here in his writings do I hold a body truer still," said the most venerable Ana de Jesús in reply to Diego's mute question. "For within them his spirit yet murmurs, as they are flesh that breathes and speaks and recites, and I hold that his verse is no less than the veins that carry his whisper. You share this view, do you not, my child?"

"As I told Your Reverence, I know naught of his verse save the Night."

"You may deny or conceal it all you like, but by my measure you are well versed in the friar's writings. Tell me, my child, do strange lines sometimes fall from your lips? Does your tongue ever cease to be your own?"

"Yes!" exclaimed Diego, feeling for the first time understood. "Soon after we from Úbeda departed did my words begin to muddle and now do they exchange themselves one for another and I end up saying naught but nonsense."

"My child, you are lovesick!"

"Me? In love? Nonsense," Diego protested, suddenly flushed.

"You are besotted!"

"I know nothing of love."

"My poor boy! Sick and mad and begging blind for those eyes in which to behold himself, a lad whose love is a secret kept even from him."

"I keep no secret but the friar's tongue," said Diego, who in trying to keep his secret let slip the secret of that other tongue from his own.

"Fear not, my child, if the meaning of Fray Juan's phrases of love escapes you when in the pitch-dark night they stream to your tongue, your mind, your flesh, your dreams, or your heart. For who could set on the page what he leads the loving souls he inhabits to understand? Who could put into words what he leads them to feel? What, moreover, he leads them to desire? No one, of course; not even those loving souls through which he passes. For this reason do these souls offer through figures, comparisons, and likenesses some part of what they feel, or else they mete out mysteries of spiritual plenitude, rather than tempt to expound it clear. And these likenesses, if not read with the spirit of love and the intelligence they bear within them, oft seem more nonsense than explanation."

"Forgive me, Your Reverence, now I fear it is not only my tongue that errs, but also my ears, for I understand nothing of what they hear."

"Do you know, my child, what Fray Juan would tell you? To love and to delight in what you do not understand."

"Then I would need to love all, for naught do I understand."

"Then a great saint would you be! But remember: this evening shall you be examined in the subject of love."

"Again, I fear I understand not what Your Reverence means."

"Dear boy, that your heart will be broken!"

"Oh, that! My heart. Broken, like in all those poems," said Diego, relieved.

"Broken?" he reconsidered.

"My heart?" he asked, now understanding.

"But tell me who will break it," he begged, now afeared.

"Tell me when," he implored, now knowing his cause lost.

"Have mercy, Your Reverence, and give me fair warning!"

"Peace, my child. I am neither sibyl nor astromancer, but a nun," said the most venerable Ana de Jesús, as if stirring from a trance. "Or do you for a vulgar procuress take me? However, if you have come to ask after the body of Fray Juan, my Sisters bade me tell you to wait here for they will not be long, though I dare say they will linger a while."

XXVII. Wherein doña Ana recites the four verses of the "Flame," several lines of which are expounded, save the sixth, which fiery demands "tear the cloth of this sweet rapport!" and as such requires its own commentary regarding whether as vestments or hymen or spiritual cloth should this fabric be understood, or perhaps as the weave of the poem itself, imploring that the text be torn so that in its laceration might its words carve a path toward presence, or whether it should be understood as all these things together, or none, for these verses are so inflamed that the more they bare themselves the more do they hide themselves and the more do their tongues of flame dazzle rather than illuminate: a secret light that blinds its witness or reader who is left uncertain and much darkened, like fire-licked matter.

The tapers were so many, so many the lanterns and so great the glow in which the night burned that the morning itself would be dazzled were it to arrive asudden.

Doña Ana had ordered the servants to gather in the chapel all the lights of the house, that she might better venerate the body of Fray Juan. And though these were most luminous and great in number, brighter still flamed the fire in her heart.

At last were the friar's words made flesh, at last was he

to her returned. After so much affliction and ailment was he to her returned, after death was he to her returned, after so much effort, so many pacts and so much gold, so many regions and distances that grew as they were crossed, and even if the next day must it be to Segovia transported, that night at least was returned to her that body most desired.

Avid, ardent, athirst did doña Ana dismiss the servants that she might with it be alone.

And there he was: exhibited in the chest wherein the nuns had arranged him, the tattered trunk of his doleful portage having been discarded, among fresh petals and green leaves of laurel that more elegant and fitting might he arrive at Segovia. Well cleansed and groomed indeed was he, yet also was he diminished, for greatly had the sisters presumed in taking as a token his remaining arm. Yet by the same secret justice that rules the balance of celestial objects and the harmony of spheres, and which dictates that there be no loss without gain, this pious subtraction did, at least, return to the body a modest symmetry.

All this did Ferrán glimpse from behind a heavy curtain. He had in secret and in darkness stolen to the chapel with his knife and his finely honed intention to filch the friar's virile pouch when he heard the servants approach with their lights and there he remained, trapped and transfixed in his hiding place.

Kneeling at the friar's feet did doña Ana begin to recite the "Flame" with such fervor that rather than sing its verses did she loudly seem to pray them:

Oh love's living flame
how gently you wound
my soul at its core!
You have quit your games,
so finish, if you would:
tear the cloth of this sweet rapport!

Though imperceptible to ordinary eyes, an artist would have recognized as Love that chubby, winged boy who shot flaming arrows from where he floated above the body of Fray Juan, and would have sketched the scene thusly. *It is a splendid thing that, since love is never idle but rather in continual motion, it is always casting flames in all directions like a blazing fire, and since its duty is to cause love and delight by its wounds, just as it resides in the soul as a living flame does it dispatch its wounds like tenderest flares of delicate love,* remarked Fray Juan in his commentary on those verses which doña Ana continued singing or pleading and which were none other but the fiery arrows shot by Love. And well pierced by the arrows of those verses did doña Ana moan:

Oh soft cautery!
Oh gratifying pain!
Oh gentle hand! Oh graceful touch
that bears eternal augury
and every debt does pay!
In killing, death as life do you couch.

Of these incandescent lines whose meaning is ignited by their recital and which move whomever tempts speak them toward moans rather than speech, writes the friar in his commentary: *To stress the sentiment and esteem with which it speaks in these four verses, the soul uses in all the exclamations, "Oh" and "how," which indicate an affectionate urging. Each time they are uttered do they reveal more of the interior than the tongue can express. "Oh" serves to express intense desire and persuasion in petitioning. The soul uses this expression for both reasons in these lines for here it suggests and stresses its tremendous desire, persuading love to release it.*

"Oh!" was Ferrán pierced by a verse.

"Oh!" did Ferrán think of Diego.

"Oh!" did Diego dream of kissing Philomela with the tongueless mouth of Fray Juan.

"Oh!" did a stag pass through Diego's dream like the line of a poem as he slumbered in the servants' quarters.

"Oh!" was this dream cut short by a knife.

"Oh!" did Diego awake to the blade of a knife and a muzzling hand that barely let him breathe.

"Oh!" did Diego glean it was the hand of Ferrán, and the blade of Ferrán, and the body of Ferrán that pressed against and oppressed his body.

"Oh!" did Diego feel the blade slide down his bare skin like a shudder and come to rest at his balls.

"Oh!" did Diego wish to say no, to beg no, please no, don't cut off my balls, don't cut off my cock, to say that he would say nothing about the friar's cock nor his tongue, that he would say nothing about anything but nothing could he say, muzzled as he was. And no longer did he wish to speak but rather to scream as he felt the knife pierce him at his core. And his soul seemed to fly from his body and it seemed he would perish. The arrow had at last met the stag, as verse met verse, and the stag did perish. Yet the stag did not perish but was turned into a dove and the dove took wing. And Diego did not perish nor was it Ferrán's knife but Ferrán's cock that did pierce and wound him thus. And thusly is the line "In killing, death as life do you couch" here expounded. And when, after wounding him, Ferrán released his grip and Diego could again open his mouth, he found he could say nothing, for nothing was there to say, save perhaps a moaned "Oh!"

> *Oh lanterns of fire*
> *in whose flickering gleam*
> *the caverns of meaning*
> *once blind and bemired*
> *now with strange art teem*
> *for their Love, warm and beaming.*

Doña Ana went on moaning these words. And the air stirred by her flights set the lantern flames aflicker. And though she continued with renewed ardor, desperation began to crackle faint in her throat.

> *So loving and fair*

do you stir in my breast,
where you alone in secret dwell,
and with your honeyed air
so glorious and blessed,
how gently you make my love swell!

Doña Ana sobbed these final words, trembling and aflame, for too late had she understood that her desire would not be satisfied. Fulfilled did it wound her deeper still and likewise did it breed more desiring. How vast the chasm that separated the friar's verses, even those she bore pierced through her heart, from the friar himself. There was the body so desired, laid before her in her home, yet more deeply did it wound her now than it had in its absence. She desired to burn inside the bones of Fray Juan, to boil in his marrow, to decompose in the dregs of his ashes, she wanted to scent his incense until she herself disappeared along with the final whiff of him, to be consumed in consuming him, for such is the voracious nature of fire. But she feared that even were she extinguished, her desire would endure.

Frightened by the blaze she called out to her brother, who arrived apace. And doña Ana begged don Luis for his aid in severing the friar's arm. As an act of revenge, consolation, justice, defeat, spite, punishment, payment, farewell, as a way of letting go of the rest, doña Ana wanted an arm. And, together, sever an arm they did.

An arm?

But Fray Juan had no arms left!

Was it not an ear, a leg, his cock?

An arm. And sometimes also a foot.

So vouch the biographers, at least.

At least, so vouches Fray Alonso de la Madre de Dios: "Once don Luis de Mercado and doña Ana had severed from the holy body an arm, and once they had removed to keep for themselves the habit and cincture he wore and had in a different habit dressed him, did they dispatch the sacred body to the monastery at Segovia with the same personages and the same secrecy by which he had been brought from Úbeda."

An arm?

Perhaps this was merely a confusion, for we have seen Fray Alonso lose his way before. Or perhaps the biographers sought to blame doña Ana for the arm taken by the nuns in Madrid. Or perhaps the nuns did not take an arm, after all. Perhaps we are the ones who are misdirected and the townfolk of Úbeda kept as compensation not an arm but rather a leg, contrary to what was stated so many pages ago. Anything is possible. There even exists one curious version defended by Fray José de Velasco, according to which the arm in doña Ana's possession was a gift from the townsfolk of Úbeda. From the townsfolk of Úbeda! When so well is it known how fervently the townsfolk of Úbeda did persevere in their dispute! Others, meanwhile, claim that doña Ana sent as a gift to Úbeda one foot wrapped with golden thread and kept the arm for herself. Who knows! Anything is possible. It is even possible that doña Ana cut from the friar an arm he no longer had; stranger things have happened. For example, there is no explaining how Ferrán, captive and concealed behind the chapel drapes, might ravage Diego from so far away.

But stranger things have happened in this shadowy world. Things more inexplicable, supernatural, secret. Wonders that cannot be reasoned, for science offers no means by which to know their meaning.

And so, lanterns means lantern, for, as the friar expounds in his commentary, all these lanterns are but one lantern which, according to its attributes and virtues, illuminates and burns as many. But lanterns also means waters, for though they were lanterns of fire, so too were they waters pure and clear.

Radiance means love which means soul which means jewel which means suffering which means virtue which means darkness which means poem which means swan which means death which means purgation which means pleasure which means wound which means hardship which means God which means bridegroom which means what fire does as it penetrates wood.

Diego means nothing.

XXVIII. Wherein, though there remain more verses than leagues ahead, this commentary declares its meagerness and insufficiency and, defeated, ends or is interrupted or remains here stammering so that the verses of Fray Juan de la Cruz might brighter shine in their own light, and so that the men might continue on their way, in their way, closing the distance that separates them from silence, from nothing, from oblivion.

The stag looked upon Diego with Diego's eyes, so near were they to one another. It had emerged out of nowhere in the midst of the forest, in the depths of the night, into the middle of the road and now was charging at the three men and their mules. Just before the collision did the stag upcast its course or flight and it seemed to soar over them before being to darkness and to nothing returned.

The bailiff crossed himself, taking this sudden appearance for the Devil's work. Ferrán gripped the hilt of his sword, late as ever. Diego cried:

> *Return, my dove,*
> *for the wounded stag*
> *now appears on the knoll*
> *in the breeze stirred by your flight . . .*

And hastened hand to mouth to quiet the untimely verse. And the bailiff and Ferrán looked upon the lad as if he were himself the stag.

"What did you just say?" demanded the bailiff.

"Nothing!" said Diego. "I said nothing! It was the friar!"

"The friar? But what nonsense is this?"

"On my honor, it was the friar's tongue stirring in my mouth!"

"The friar's tongue?"

"I'll tear out your friar's tongue if you keep up this foolery!" threatened Ferrán, feeling himself under threat.

"Enough! Silence, the lot of you!" sliced the bailiff, exasperated by the unfathomable.

Not another word did Diego speak. Silent, eager, exhausted, their way lit only by the moon, the three men continued along their arduous path, hastening their journey's end. Though more pleasant and restful would it have been to have taken two nights, the bailiff had insisted on hurrying this final stretch into a single day to risk less the unforeseen, their task being so near its completion. And so, with what remained of the body of Fray Juan in a wooden chest, they set out from Madrid at daybreak and were by then so deep in the night that they were likely no more than a league from Segovia.

Near a large rock formation, Diego fancied that he saw himself wandering through the dark in pursuit of that dubious stag but, as his impulse to bid himself farewell was muzzled, he said nothing at all, for though they traveled in the strictest silence, Ferrán did often take advantage of the bailiff's distraction to show Diego the blade of his knife and thus quietly did he communicate.

What mute words proffered this tongue of steel? Stern, it ordered Diego to silence, threatening mutilation if he disobeyed. But might the blade not also be interpreted as Ferrán's cock promising Diego another loving wound? Anything could mean anything, for, as has been said, objects, signs, and words had long ago come unbound and, released from their stays, unhinged did wander through forms and shift among figures. And so, Ferrán's insistent blade, glinting in the pale moonlight, could just as likely be violently threatening or gladly promising or sadly or solemnly announcing the separation of those three men who had been the arms and legs of a single purpose which would soon be dismembered like the body of a saint.

Huzzah! Huzzah!

Before their eyes, under the red glow of dawn, the city of Segovia rose majestic from the base of the mountains.

Oh wondrous delight!

Oh triumphant daybreak, that morning in May!

The bailiff crossed himself, giving mute thanks to the heavens. Ferrán sheathed his knife. Diego opened his mouth but could not say a word, as if transformed into Philomela he was readying his silent song.

The moon lingered in the firmament like a relic of that endless month of difficult, delirious, terrifying, mysterious, loving, perplexing, pitch-dark nights that were now but the memory of one single night turned morning.

The moon: a slow host dissolving on the tongue of day.

Printed in the USA
CPSIA information can be obtained
at www.ICGtesting.com
JSHW082047030823
45874JS00004B/5

9 781646 052790